The Homework

STRIKE

GREG PINCUS

The Homework STRIKE

SCHOLASTIC INC.

Arthur A. Levine Books hardcover edition designed by Nina Goffi, published by Arthur A. Levine Books, an imprint of Scholastic Inc., January 2017.

All rights reserved. Published by Scholastic Inc., *Publishers since 1920*. SCHOLASTIC, the LANTERN LOGO, and associated logos are trademarks and/or registered trademarks of Scholastic Inc.

ISBN 978-0-439-91302-7

10 9 8 7 6 5 4 3 2   19 20 21 22

Printed in the U.S.A.   40

This edition first printing 2018

Book design by Nina Goffi

For Mom
and Dad

History's a mystery.

Science is a curse.

My English grade could use some aid —

My math one's even worse.

 My Spanish skill is nearly nil.

PE's like a punch.

The only class I think I'll pass

in middle school is lunch!

1

Maple syrup is good on pancakes, but it's really terrible on homework.

Gregory K. was reminded of this simple fact as he hurried to finish a sheet of math problems while devouring breakfast — and dripping syrup — at the same time.

"Ugh. Right on the three problems I've already done," Gregory moaned as he grabbed a napkin. "What are the odds?"

"The odds are terrible," his older brother, O, said from the far end of the dining room table, "since the odds were poor that you really got three problems done in the first place. Oh. Wait. You didn't say got them done right."

Gregory rubbed the napkin on the spill, leaving big chunks of shredded paper behind on his homework.

"You know," his younger sister, Kay, chimed in, peering over the cover of *Harry Potter and the Deathly Hallows*, "if you just add some bacon and eggs to that page, you could feed it to the dog and you'd have the perfect homework excuse."

"He has the perfect excuse already." O smiled. "He's Gregory K."

"My perfect excuse is that I have to live with you," Gregory said as he dripped water onto the homework sheet in an attempt to de-napkinize it.

"Believe what you want to believe, little brother." O grabbed his own plate and headed into the kitchen. "And by the way, 212, 397, 11 with remainder 4, 22, 3, 14, 6.2, 9.9, 10, and 14. You're welcome."

Gregory glared at his brother until he was no longer in sight, then quickly grabbed his pencil from the tabletop and wrote frantically on his wet, sticky homework.

"You don't really believe those were the right answers, do you?" Kay asked her scribbling brother.

"I do. He saw me without my pencil and dealing with syrup. What better time to mess with me?" Gregory drummed his pencil on the table. "Do you remember the fifth answer?"

Kay returned to her reading with a look that made Gregory wish he'd never gotten out of bed that morning. He stared at the homework, pencil hovering in the air. And then Gregory tossed the pencil aside, grabbed the syrup bottle, and poured a huge puddle onto the paper.

"I saw that, you know," Kay said, even though her eyes never left the book page. How she could always do that, Gregory had never figured out, chalking it up to "little sister power" or something.

"Just don't tell Mom, okay?" Gregory looked at his sister with big puppy dog eyes as he smeared the syrup around, adding some extra ripped napkin pieces for good measure.

"Your secret's safe with me," Kay said, still engrossed in her book. "But trust me. You need to practice that look in the mirror. It's not conveying what you want it to."

Maybe it wasn't, Gregory thought, and maybe he needed to look in a mirror at some point, but at the moment he didn't care—his secret was safe and his homework was finished, at least if you defined "finished" as no longer waiting to be done.

Gregory K. walked to school waving his homework in the wind to dry it. As he headed up the long hill to Morris Champlin Middle School, his friend Alex fell into step beside him, untied shoelaces clicking rhythmically against the sidewalk.

"Dude," Alex said, "it's too early in the morning to be waving the surrender flag."

"It's my math, and I surrendered years ago." Gregory brushed his hair out of his eyes with his free hand. "Did you get your history done?"

"Finished at the crack of midnight, my friend. You?" Alex popped his knuckles as they walked on.

"Did it with Ana and Benny. Most of it, anyway. You shoulda been there."

"I was doing math with my tutor, then the bonus Spanish lesson that I never asked for. But it's all good."

The two climbed the hill in silence for a moment, the morning sun smiling down on their frowning faces.

"You know what I don't understand?" Gregory asked. "How do the popular kids have time to be popular? I mean, since seventh grade started, I haven't had time to do anything but schoolwork. But they're all doing sports and hanging out at the mall and going to parties and just standing in the hall being all popular and stuff. Maybe they don't sleep?"

"They're all vampires, dude. And to them, you and me are like redshirts on *Star Trek*." Alex grinned. "I think that's my next essay for the newspaper right there."

"What is? How you can mix pop culture references to confuse everyone?"

"You should join the paper. Have a poetry column." Alex leapt over a crack in the sidewalk, his gangly legs seeming to go in four different directions at once.

"Like anyone would read that?" Gregory kicked a rock up the hill. "Anyway, I promised Kelly I'd finish up my book. So if I get free time, that's what I do."

"And . . . ?" Alex looked expectantly at his friend.

"So little time, so little progress." Without breaking stride, Gregory folded his homework in half and swung his backpack off one shoulder to put the paper inside. "Kinda like the film series you were going to make."

"Yeah. That's not happening, unless 'series' means twelve seconds of one film. Then I totally win. But we're talking about your writing here," Alex said.

"It's no different. You make great stuff. Or you made great stuff. Now . . . poof." Gregory pantomimed blowing away an imaginary object.

"I'm just busy with other cool stuff, you know? But you not writing is you not being Gregory K."

Over the past summer, Gregory and his best friend, Kelly, had gone to Author's Camp, and it had been the best experience of their lives. They took classes from professional writers, they hung out with other kids who loved to write as much as they did, and they got to see each other for the first time since Kelly had moved away at the end of sixth grade. Sure, it had only been four weeks since she'd moved, but that was the longest time they'd gone without seeing each other since they'd been in the same baby group before they could even speak, let alone write.

At camp, Gregory had written poetry and short stories, and he'd realized that they all worked together. He promised Kelly that he'd keep writing and turn them into a book, even if the only person who ever read it was her. Kelly had been working on a novel and had also promised to keep writing and be done before their next school year finished. When camp ended, they were both convinced that they knew what they were going to do with their lives. They were going to be writers, because, well, there didn't need to be an explanation. It was just obvious.

At the end of the summer, Gregory had still been writing full steam ahead. Once seventh grade started, though, time became harder to find. So did energy. And as the first month of school passed and he struggled to keep up with math and history and science and social studies and Spanish and PE, the idea that he should spend time writing became harder to accept in his own head. It's not that he thought he was a bad writer — he had won the Best Metaphor Award at camp, after all — but really . . . what was the point of writing when there were all these things he had to deal with that seemed so important to everyone else?

If Kelly still lived in town, Gregory imagined that he'd talk with her about this and she'd kick him in the calf and tell him to stop being silly. But she wasn't here, and he didn't feel like he could talk with Ana, Alex, or Benny about writing the way he talked with Kelly. So he didn't. Instead, he went to school, did his homework, and promised himself that if there was any time left in the day, he'd pull out his notebook to write. But there was never really time.

"Dude," Alex said, bringing Gregory out of his thoughts, "Bankster alert!"

The two boys were now almost at the school, a big brick behemoth that glowered down on the town from atop its hilly perch. Students were getting out of parents' cars, arriving on foot and by bike, and hanging out all around the neat green yard in front of the main doors. There was a constant buzz of conversation and laughter before the long day ahead.

But moving through that buzz was a pocket of silence . . . a silence that traveled with Dr. Bankster, their seventh-grade history teacher, as he walked from his car to the front doors of the school.

Gregory and Alex watched their teacher move along—a slow, steady pace with an almost impercepti-ble limp—and saw their schoolmates stop speaking, sometimes mid-word, as he drew near. Although he always wore a suit and bow tie, Dr. Bankster wasn't really an imposing figure. In fact, most of the eighth graders were taller than he was, and his remaining wisps of white hair often blew around in the wind and made him look silly, not scary. Still, everyone knew that he was the most demanding—some would say unforgiving—teacher you'd have in your entire middle school experience. In fact, Gregory's father said that Dr. Bankster was the toughest teacher he had in his entire life, including college and graduate school.

The students' quiet, Gregory knew, came from a mix of respect and fear and an undercurrent of feeling judged, somehow, as though the good doctor would frown upon whatever they were saying or how they were saying it. Then as Dr. Bankster passed by, conversations resumed . . . and the silence moved forward step by step.

"How old do you think he is?" Alex asked as the teacher entered the school, disappearing from sight.

"One hundred fifteen," Gregory replied without hesitating. "That's why he teaches history. Because he lived it."

"I bet he invented homework," Alex said as he led the way into school.

"Nah. But he perfected it. No question about that." Gregory felt the sunlight fading away as he passed the threshold of the school.

Morris Champlin was an old building, and the

high-ceilinged hallways were lit by long, glowing fluorescent bulbs that made everyone and everything look a little too yellow. The classrooms, though, had big windows and good natural light. None were as bright as Dr. Bankster's room, and that's where Gregory and Alex's school day began. So, with backpacks bearing down on them, the two friends took a sharp right and began the long climb to the history room—the only classroom on the fourth floor of the school.

Dr. Bankster's classroom was a simple square that sat on the rooftop, and it had been his space for over thirty years now. He kept the windows as clean as could be, and on sunny days like today, his room was bright and happy. The kids in his room, however, were usually tense and unhappy at worst or unsettled at best, because Dr. B. was well-known for his surprise assignments, almost always in the form of essay questions.

The essays could be assigned at any time and were graded on content, grammar, and clarity. The rumor was that no one had ever gotten an A on an essay, and that had certainly proven true so far this year. So with the essay possibility always dangling in the air, students stayed on edge, even when their teacher was giving a lecture or showing a movie or doing one of his famous (or infamous depending on who you asked) "history alive" lessons. Tension constantly filled the air, although Dr. Bankster never acknowledged it. He just taught, his dark blue eyes sweeping the classroom and making contact with everyone, seemingly all at the same time.

Unlike his classmates, though, Gregory was not tense in history class. The essays didn't scare him, even though he hadn't yet gotten an A on one. The subject matter was not his favorite, true, but American history wasn't bad, and it was clear that this was a teacher who loved what he taught and would answer students' questions with a passion that could actually excite you about things like the Smoot-Hawley Tariff Act.

In fact, history class would've been Gregory's favorite except for two things: It was an exhausting way to start the day, since Dr. Bankster didn't believe in downtime . . . and he definitely believed in homework.

Every day, students left history with multiple assignments. There was always additional reading beyond the class text and a single paragraph of writing due every day. Sometimes there was a work sheet to do or a map to draw or questions to prepare for the next day's class. There were also optional assignments you could choose to do for extra credit—more writing, lengthier texts, videos online with essay responses—and a choice of embarking on longer-term projects for even more extra credit.

In the history of Dr. Bankster's class, only one student had done every possible assignment, and that was Gregory's older brother, O. Most mere student-mortals like Gregory did the bare minimum . . . though even that took him forty-five minutes or more on most nights. And most mere student-mortals set their sights on getting a B at maximum . . . and to get that B, they'd probably have to do a lot of extra credit.

For years, parents had complained about Dr. Bankster's grading, but he laughed off the issue. "If I gave everyone an A, what would it mean? It would mean it was time for me to retire," he said. And then he'd repeat his mantra: "A grade is earned, not given." Gregory was currently earning a C– in history, and, frankly, he was okay with that.

Today in class, Gregory's mind wasn't focused on his grade. Instead, it was focused on tea.

"Do you smell that aroma?" Dr. Bankster asked as he walked around the classroom with a large and very fragrant bag of loose-leaf tea. "That is tea. Not that watered-down stuff you get at restaurants when you order iced tea. Oh no. This is what you kids might call the good stuff, and it is part of your history. Because this is the same type of tea that the colonists drank, sent over from England where they had known it well."

Dr. Bankster returned to the front of the classroom as an electric kettle whistled for his attention.

"Ahhh, yes. This tea is wonderful. It is more than a beverage. It is an experience — steeping it, drinking it, appreciating its past. As a special treat today, I will make anyone in here a cup of tea. And to try to show you how meaningful a part of life tea was in the past, if you have a cup, you are excused from homework for this week." The class buzzed excitedly. The smell of tea still hung in the air, now promising great rewards.

"There's just one thing," the good doctor continued, and the class fell silent. "A cup's worth of tea is precious to me. So for each cup's worth of my tea you take from me, I will lower your current overall numerical grade by three full points. I quickly add that you should remember that the first grading period ends this week. You may not appeal this decision to anyone.

You have no choice in how this works, as the tea and rules are mine."

Gregory looked around the room as his classmates digested the news. He spotted his friend Ana quickly scribbling on her notebook while nervously chewing her hair, and he knew that she was trying to figure out if this was a good deal. Other students were doing the math too, trying to determine how much time they'd save by not doing homework, how much time they'd spend on extra-credit work if they needed to regain those three points, and how much the missing week of homework would normally cost their average anyway. One after another they put their pencils down, often slamming them with frustration. Dr. Bankster stood at the front of the room, carefully measuring a single cup's worth of loose tea into a strainer, ready to brew.

Besides the fact that the actual math was beyond him, Gregory didn't check the numbers because he knew beyond a shadow of a doubt that it was a terrible deal overall. While he might struggle a bit with history itself, Gregory already had a good sense of his teacher, and he knew that Dr. Bankster was doing this to illustrate a point, not to help anyone out. This instinct was also confirmed by looking over to Alex and seeing his friend give him a subtle shake no.

Mutterings of disappointment filled the classroom. Dr. Bankster held up his teakettle. "Anyone? Anyone? It's truly wonderful tea."

Suddenly, Gregory sat bolt upright in his chair. He'd figured out what his teacher was doing, and he saw an opportunity of pure upside potential. As he raised his hand, Gregory noted a dull, familiar ache in his calf. His friend Kelly had kicked him there under tables and desks for years as a warning whenever Gregory had started pursuing one of his offbeat ideas. Even now that she was gone, the dull ache would still pop up like a finely tuned alarm. Some days, that pain would make him stop in his tracks.

Today was not one of those days.

"Yes, Gregory Korenstein-Jasperton?" Dr. Bankster said. "Would you like a cup of tea?"

"No, sir. I just had something to say." Gregory gulped nervously.

"And what might that be?" Dr. Bankster calmly watched his student.

Gregory jumped up from his seat, dashed to the

front of the room, grabbed the strainer full of loose tea with his right hand, and ran to the window. As he ran, he yelled, "No taxation without representation! No taxation without representation!"

His fellow students gasped and oohed as Gregory opened a window along the side of the room and flung the tea outside. The loose leaves fluttered quickly over the side of the building, disappearing from view.

"It's the Morris Champlin Middle School Tea Party! Pretend that's the harbor out there," Gregory said as triumphantly as he could.

For a moment Gregory thought he'd seen a hint of a smile play across Dr. Bankster's jowly face, but the first words out of his teacher's mouth came with no hint of approval.

"Oh, dear. I am missing a cup's worth of tea. Would any of you care to tell me who took it?" Dr. Bankster looked out at the rest of the class. "By the way, if I get no answer, you will all lose three points from your grade."

Alex leapt to his feet. "It was him!" Alex pointed at a cutout of the school mascot, Mo the Bear, tacked on the wall. Other kids in the class laughed, but within a few moments, at least fifteen fingers were pointed directly at Gregory. Alex shrugged and sat back down. "I gotta get to the eye doctor."

"Ahh, the guilty party," Dr. Bankster said with over-the-top glee. "You made two poor choices, Gregory K. You did not act under cover of darkness, and you did not conspire with a supportive group of like-minded individuals who would share in the upside you would gain for your actions."

Carefully putting the kettle down, Dr. Bankster shuffled over to his desk and pulled his leather-bound grade book from the top drawer. He placed it on the desktop and flipped it open. Then the teacher reached into his pocket, and the whole class leaned forward. Gregory's calf ached as he watched and waited. In that pocket lived two pens—one blue and one red—and only one of them meant good news. Gregory hoped his cleverness would be rewarded amply.

"Awww, really?" Gregory involuntarily squeaked out when the red pen emerged from Dr. Bankster's pocket.

"I do admire your bravery, but you cannot appeal this decision, and whining about it will not help, Mr. Korenstein-Jasperton. On the plus side, you may take the rest of this week off from homework in this class." Dr. Bankster used the red pen to change Gregory's average in the grade book. The whole class cringed in sympathy. "And if you would like to do some extra-credit work to raise your grade . . . and looking at it now, you might wish to do that . . . you know the assignments are available."

The sound of the grade book being closed seemed to echo around his head. This was math Gregory could do — he now had a D. And it wasn't fair! He'd shown his knowledge of history and played off his teacher's ideas, yet he still was punished. That was all kinds of wrong.

"You were NOT punished, Gregory K.," his friend Ana said to him as he joined her and Benny for their daily "homework club" after school, today at Ana's apartment. "You got what was coming to you."

"Yeah, yeah. I know. But I helped make his lesson better, didn't I? I should get something for that!" Gregory tried to drown his frustration with a chocolate chip cookie dunked in milk. It helped, though only a little. It would probably take a number of dunks and bites to feel fully better.

"You looked for opportunity where none was offered. Statistically, that's a bad risk." Benny shook his head and pointed to his T-shirt, which bore the words *Think Outside the Quadrilateral Parallelogram* over an image of a cube. "This is good advice, but incomplete since most people you'll encounter do not do the same. They are stuck in the box, and therefore, so are you."

"I don't even see the box until it's too late." Gregory sighed. "You guys wanna start with math today?"

The three friends reached into their backpacks and pulled out math textbooks. The trio—often a quartet with Alex, when he wasn't working for the school paper or dealing with the array of tutors his parents hired to help "get the most" out of him—had been gathering to do homework together almost every day after school since the second week of seventh grade. They rotated between each other's places and usually worked together right until dinnertime, then finished their work on their own later.

Gregory was the English star, Benny rocked science, Alex was the math expert, and Ana . . . well . . . she actually seemed to struggle a bit with all of it. But they knew they did better together than on their own.

In fact, on the days after they didn't meet up, Gregory far more frequently ended up doing things like spilling massive quantities of maple syrup as part of his homework completion strategy.

Benny and Gregory had known each other for years, and Gregory felt that Benny was like a nice version of O, though with a buzz cut and an endless supply of funny T-shirts. They hadn't been close friends in the early years, but as they'd gotten older, Gregory had realized how smart and funny Benny was, even if no one else in class fully appreciated the humor. Plus, Benny's mom made the most amazing dumplings—from chicken to fish to veggie to dessert varieties inspired by recipes from all around the world—so that didn't hurt.

Ana had a streak of blue in her otherwise jet-black hair, wore boots with a dress and leggings every day, and had three earrings in her left ear but only one in her right. She was also new to town and had been wandering alone in the cafeteria on the first day of school this year when Gregory saw her. He sensed a lot of loneliness and fear beneath Ana's tough, direct exterior, and he'd thought of Kelly starting a new school 144 miles away and hoped someone befriended her.

So he'd decided he would befriend Ana. Turns out, she was nice and funny and loved pop culture and, just like Gregory and his existing friends, didn't really fit in anywhere in the great middle school hierarchy of groups. She was just Ana, and that worked for her and her new homework friends.

Together, the three slogged through their math. Or really, Gregory slogged while Benny flew and Ana moved steadily, but being with the others helped them all stay on task, and that was good because when Gregory was confronted with a sheet of math problems, his instinct was to run away. A typical pass through a work sheet would take Gregory hours on his own, but in the group, they allotted thirty minutes, and by staying focused and asking for help, he could almost always get close enough to done that he'd get a passing grade on the homework.

Today was no exception, although he didn't even ask for help. That was because as he stared at a problem and began drumming his pencil on the table, Benny looked over and said, "Flip the numerator and denominator," which was not only the help he needed but totally cool because Benny was seeing it upside down and somehow knew that things weren't flipped. Gregory couldn't even figure that out right side up!

Gregory followed Benny's advice, went back and corrected two other problems, and slowly pushed forward.

"Science time," Ana announced as she came back from the kitchen with another plate of cookies. Even though there often wasn't enough time to finish a class's work, Ana made sure the group moved on every half hour. This was partly because of her belief that it would be better to get some work done for each class rather than all the work for one or two of the classes, and partly for a practical reason — her mother worked out of the house and her father worked at home, but his kitchen skills were, according to Ana, "one step above disaster." So she cooked the family dinner every single night and wanted to be done with homework by six to prepare it. That meant they couldn't drift beyond two hours total, and with four core subjects, they had to move on regularly whether they finished the day's work or not. Gregory usually didn't finish everything, but just like with the math work sheet, he finished enough to get by or finish it at home later.

"I miss elementary school," Gregory said as he swapped his math book for his science book. "Or at least the lighter workload."

"I have a theory that they removed two hours from

the day this summer while we weren't looking," Benny chimed in. "That would explain why I no longer have time for reading for pleasure, watching TV, or practicing violin."

"You said you always hated violin," Gregory said.

"I do. But I dislike my mother's constant nagging me to practice even more," Benny said. Gregory laughed, since Benny's mom seemed like one of the nicest people ever, and it was hard to imagine her nagging. Still, Benny's deadpan look made Gregory wonder if it was a joke.

"Whatever I used to do," Ana said as she placed the cookies on the table and sat down, "it was more fun than this. No insult."

"None taken," Gregory said as he grabbed a cookie. "I'm gonna cut out when you guys start history today, okay? I might as well take advantage of not having to do the work."

"You have to do the extra credit, Gregory K.," Benny said seriously. "You have a D, and you only have a week to address that."

"Well, I'm gonna have a D, then. To gain three points, it's probably, what, ten extra hours of homework? Maybe more, and I don't have time for that this week. It's the big open mic thing at Booktastic on Friday night, and I've gotta get ready for that. I'm even going to try and write a new poem just for it."

Booktastic was the indie bookstore in the neighboring town about twenty miles away—there hadn't been one in Gregory's city for nearly ten years—and it was one of his favorite places on earth. The open mic nights were always great, and full of writing friends he rarely got to see. Plus, sometimes amazing authors who were celebrities to him stopped in to perform. He'd also had a well-published poet ask for his autograph after he'd read his own poems aloud! He hadn't missed an open mic night in a long time, and he wasn't about to start because of homework.

In early spring, Elton Edwards, Gregory and Kelly's favorite poet and novelist (who had been a guest speaker at Author's Camp over the past summer) was going to do an event at Booktastic. Gregory had saved his allowance to buy a ticket to the small after-reading conversation and for four books to be signed. Kelly had a ticket too, and Gregory had circled the day in his brain's calendar since the moment it was announced. On bad days at school, thinking about an upcoming open mic night would get him through. On really bad days, he'd think of Elton Edwards. Today had only been bad, so the open mic night was all that was on his mind.

"If I had a D, my parents would keep me in the house forever. And . . ." Benny paused mid-thought. "Your parents don't know, do they?"

"Of course not! It just happened today," Gregory said. "And I'll raise it soon, so there's nothing to worry about."

His friends looked at him dubiously, and Gregory tried to put on a brave face. But the truth was, he'd never even thought about the fact that he now had a D and that that D could have an impact on his life. He decided to put it out of his mind. For once, he was grateful to have homework to do to keep him busy. He dove into science, pushed through English, then left when the group switched to history.

On the way home, Gregory had a spring in his step. No history homework meant forty-five minutes to work on his writing, the stuff that made him happy and had seemed so important just a month ago. Tonight, he knew, was going to be a good night. He picked up the pace to get home faster.

The moment Gregory entered his house, he could

smell trouble, although that was because it was what his mom had dubbed "Mix It Up Monday!," when different members of the family took charge of dinner. This was O's week, and that meant something was going to be burning . . . which was true even if the plan was for cold leftovers. Gregory thought O tried to cause trouble to avoid having to make dinner, but his parents had watched and realized O simply had no idea what he was doing in the kitchen.

It turned out, though, that the real trouble came from a different direction.

"I checked your grades on the ParentPortal site today, Gregory," his mom said as the whole family sat down to plates of burned baked beans and burned rice. Her hair was pulled back, revealing a pencil still tucked behind her ear, even though she'd been home from her accounting job for more than an hour.

"You said your password didn't work!" Gregory shouted louder than he'd meant to. His stomach tied up in knots despite the fact he hadn't sampled the food yet.

"I got a new password. I think you know how that works. Now, we talked about this before the school year started. I'm sorry to say that if those are your grades at the end of this week, then you'll be grounded." His mom's tone was firm, not angry. But to Gregory, it felt like a dagger.

"What? That's not fair! Report cards aren't even out yet."

"Like that'll make it better," O said quietly.

"The quarter ends Friday, Gregory. Those are your grades. We discussed this multiple times, and I think it was clear." His mom was often no-nonsense, but tonight, it seemed to Gregory, she was even more so.

"Mom. Friday night . . ." Gregory started, but his father interrupted.

"I know the open mic night is very important to you, Gregory. But your grades are important to us," his dad said, a hint of frustration in his voice. He looked at his son over his glasses, which had slid partway down his nose.

"You can't be serious," Gregory moaned. "I've gotta be there. What do you want me to do?"

"No Ds was what we said. So raise your history grade," his mother said simply.

"That was a pretty obvious answer, don't you think?" his dad added oh-so-helpfully.

"I've passed every test," Gregory protested. "I'm learning stuff! Isn't that what matters?"

"A deal's a deal, Gregory." His mother's tone made it clear the conversation was over. The family sat in uncomfortable tension with the only sounds coming from O crunching rice and Kay's fork dragging over her plate as she mixed the rice and beans.

"Would this be the wrong time," Kay asked after a long pause, "for me to mention that I got a 107 on my math test today?"

If anyone else had said that, it would have upset Gregory, even though he knew Kay's success was unrelated to his failure. But he also knew that of all the people in the family, she was the only one who would see his side here. If he had a side, that is.

As conversation resumed at the table, Gregory stayed silent, trying to think. Maybe he could do enough extra credit to raise his grade in history... though Dr. Bankster's bonus assignments were long and not designed to be done very fast. Maybe if he skipped all his other homework, called in sick to school, gave up sleep, and got really lucky?

Maybe he could've done it, Gregory thought, if he had started the extra credit work right after school like Benny had tried to tell him to do. And clearly, he shouldn't have done what he did in history class.

But he'd done it. He couldn't turn back time. So there was really only one thing to do to solve his current problem.

He needed to hack into the ParentPortal site and change his grade, lock his teacher out of it, then steal Dr. Bankster's grade book to eliminate any evidence.

That didn't seem possible, though, nor smart nor the right thing to do. But the whole situation felt so unfair — if it weren't for all the homework he had to do, he'd actually have better grades and time to do extra credit! He'd be going to open mic night and working on his own writing. The writing he did for Kelly. And for himself.

Now none of that was going to happen. Unless . . .

Yes. Unless. As Dr. Seuss had taught him in *The Lorax*, there was always an *unless*. He just had to figure out what it was this time.

Gregory asked to be excused, then hurried to his room. He was a man on a mission, and nothing would stop him. Unless . . .

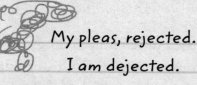

2

My pleas, rejected.
I am dejected.
My plans, confounded —
I have been grounded.

"Dude," Alex said as he rode his skateboard alongside Gregory on the way to school the next morning, "you are not going to win an argument with Dr. B. Just. Give. That. Up. Now."

"Do you see any other options for me?" Gregory asked. "I mean, we did the math, right? I've got a valid point."

"I don't think he'll see it that way." Alex pushed his way slowly up the steep grade to Morris Champlin. "Your plan is as bad as my plan to skateboard uphill."

"Mine's probably worse," Gregory admitted. "Do you think I can bribe him, maybe?"

"I'm thinking the only thing he'd want is permission to toy with your grade," Alex said, "and, uh, well, you already gave him that, GK."

"There's not another open mic night for months! I'm desperate, Alex. Like seriously desperate."

"Considering you're going to his office hours before school, I kinda figured that out," Alex said with a laugh. The way the boys had heard the story was that in the last twenty-five years, no one had ever gone to Dr. Bankster's morning office hours, which were held twice weekly, because the people who used to go always failed the class in the end, as though Dr. B. was picking on them. Relentlessly and demoralizingly picking on them. Some of the last people who went to office hours, the boys had heard, dropped out of school and were never heard from again. Gregory wasn't sure that last part was true, though no one ever went to Dr. Bankster's office hours just the same. Still, desperate times called for desperate measures.

Morris Champlin loomed ahead, far quieter fifteen minutes earlier than the friends normally arrived. Yet even now, it looked like middle school, a bunch of small cliques already formed: the jocks; the crew who looked like they spent more time on their hair and clothes each day than Gregory did each month; the gamers off in the shade, far from the group of kids who were somehow at the top of the social strata just by existing. No one paid attention to any group but their own, and today no one even acknowledged Gregory and Alex arriving.

"I could really learn to hate this place," Gregory muttered.

"Luckily it's only two years of your life!" Alex said with both thumbs raised and a goofy smile on his face.

"Wish me luck," Gregory said as he headed toward the front doors.

"I'm just hoping you come back with your head still on, dude." Alex watched Gregory pull open the front doors and head inside. "And hey! Good luck!"

Gregory trudged slowly up the stairs, breathing deeply and trying to calm his nerves. He'd practiced what he was going to say for most of the night, even using the time he might have written or finished his other homework to make sure he could make a good argument. A desperate argument, perhaps, but missing open mic night was not acceptable.

His backpack got heavier and heavier as he rose up

the stairs. By the time he reached the third floor, the noises from below had faded away, and he could hear his heart pounding. Gregory steeled himself for the final flight, then started up.

Gregory got to the first landing on the stairs and rounded a corner to continue to the top. Above him he could see Dr. Bankster's classroom door. At the sight of it, he turned around and hurried back down to the third floor, breathing quickly. This was not going to be easy.

Suddenly, the silence was broken by the squeaking of the door one flight above him. Footsteps fell on the stairs, and Gregory started to panic—he'd planned to be safe in the classroom when he talked to Dr. Bankster, not out in the open. Gregory didn't know whether to run away or hurry up to the midflight landing to intercept his teacher. Instead, he simply froze in place, eyes locked on the landing at the bend in the stairs.

He saw Ana on the landing before she saw him. There was enough time that he could've gotten out of sight, but Gregory was too startled.

"Morning, Gregory K.," Ana said as she came downstairs toward him, her boots clunking as she walked.

"What are you doing here?" Gregory asked incredulously. She still had her head attached, he noticed, and at least that was a positive sign. But still . . . what was she doing here?

"Uh . . . going to Dr. Bankster's office hours, just like you, right?" Ana stopped beside Gregory when she reached the third floor.

"I forgot. You're new here," Gregory said. "You don't know the history."

"And if I knew the history, I wouldn't need to see Dr. B." Ana smiled as she gave Gregory a bump with her shoulder to drive the joke home. She headed for the stairs down. "Good luck up there!"

Gregory watched Ana go. Her leggings matched her hair, he realized, which was pretty cool, but running into her this morning had totally shaken his focus. Still, Ana had survived her brush with Bankster, so maybe, just maybe, there was more hope than he'd expected.

Holding his backpack strap tightly, Gregory started up that final staircase. He knew this time, there'd be no turning back. He only hoped he'd be able to walk back down on his own power.

Gregory opened the door to Dr. Bankster's class-room and was immediately greeted by his teacher.

"Gregory K., I am surprised to see you here," Dr. Bankster said from behind his desk.

"And I'm surprised to be here," Gregory admitted.

"What can I do for you this morning?" Dr. Bankster indicated a seat opposite his desk. Gregory walked over.

"I think my grade is unfair, and I wanted to talk about it. Sir. Dr. Bankster, sir." Gregory breathed a sigh of relief as he sat down. At least he'd said what he'd wanted to say.

"You are not the first student I've heard say that, nor will you be the last," Dr. Bankster replied. "Why do you think it is unfair? The three-point deduction from yesterday, perhaps?"

"Not really. I mean, I thought what I did was kinda cool, but you hadn't said that role-play would change anything, and I took a cup's worth of tea," Gregory said. "Although if you want to give the points back, I won't stop you."

"I appreciated how you helped me illustrate my points, yes, but breaking the rules always has consequences," Dr. Bankster continued. "Which was another one of the points of the lesson, that I was able to illustrate by running the blade of my pen through the heart of your grade point average."

"Ouch."

"I am sure. So if not the three points, Gregory K., what do you find unfair?" Dr. Bankster reached toward the floor beside his chair and pulled up his teakettle. "Tea?" he asked as he opened up a desk drawer and pulled out a mug.

"No, thank you," Gregory replied. With a deep breath he continued. "I am doing well on your tests and doing well on the surprise essays, and I am participating in class. I'm not getting an A, I know . . ."

"Your brother did, of course. Quite an . . . an . . . an interesting student he was. But do go on." Dr. Bankster poured himself a mug of tea as he listened.

"I'd be getting a C based on all that. A high C. The thing that's lowering my grade is my homework." Gregory pulled a sheet of paper from his back pocket and unfolded it, smoothing it on the desk. "If you'll look at this, you'll see that homework brought my grade down so that yesterday's mess gave me a D.

I don't think that's fair. I'm learning what you're teaching, Dr. Bankster. Isn't that the point?"

Dr. Bankster looked at the paper Gregory had put on his desk. "This is interesting. Did you figure this out yourself?"

"Alex helped me. Math is not my strong suit," Gregory admitted.

"Mine neither," Dr. Bankster replied. "But no matter. I'll trust the math you're presenting."

As Dr. Bankster paused, Gregory was filled with hope. Math, of all things, was making his case for him. Images of open mic night danced in his head. He'd be there, unless . . .

"If you are not completing your homework and it is lowering your grade to the point where you are in trouble and you are just talking to me now, then you are not learning everything I am teaching, Mr. Korenstein-Jasperton," Dr. Bankster said simply. "There is a reason for every assignment I give."

"I didn't say there wasn't," Gregory protested.

"No, you did not. But listen to me well—there is a reason for the homework. There is something I am trying to teach you. It is that simple." Dr. Bankster sipped his tea. Gregory knew the conversation should be over now. He knew he should get up and leave. Instead, he pushed the sheet of math toward his teacher again.

"Is the reason for the homework just to upset kids? Is it to make me miss out on something really important? I just don't get it. I really don't, Dr. Bankster." Gregory stood up, grabbed his backpack, and headed to the door. As he opened it, Dr. Bankster spoke again.

"The answer is in history, Gregory K.," Dr. Bankster said calmly. "I am confident that you can figure it out."

Gregory turned to look back at his teacher to see if there was a look of smugness or sarcasm on his face, but instead he was met by Bankster's dark blue eyes almost twinkling back at him.

"Those who ignore history are doomed to repeat it, after all," Dr. Bankster added.

"And those who ignore history homework are doomed to repeat history class," Gregory grumbled as he left the room. Dr. Bankster's laughter echoed after him.

"That's fabulous!" Dr. Bankster said through his laughs. "I'm so glad you came by. See you in a few minutes!"

Gregory closed the door and hurried down the

steps. A giant "unless" had been flung in front of him, and all he wanted to do was go hide under the covers at home safe in bed. Instead, he had to wait for the morning bell to ring . . . and then get through a day of school.

"There's no hope," Gregory K. said as he lay on the floor beneath Benny's dining room table. Somehow, he'd made it through the day, but here with Alex, Ana, and Benny after school, the flood of emotion was too much. "I hate homework. I hate it."

"Gee, and here I thought I was the only one," Ana said from a chair above him.

"What does he even mean, 'the answer is in history'? The answer is that teachers are getting revenge because they had to do homework when they were our age." Gregory reached a hand up from the floor, and Benny placed a shrimp dumpling in it. "That's why we do homework."

"I dunno, dude. I thought it was to teach us work habits and stuff," Alex offered up as he dipped his own dumpling in a deep brown sauce.

"And help us learn," Ana said.

"Reinforce the day's lesson," Alex said between bites of food.

"Teach us more material," Benny said.

"Plus, keep us out of trouble," Ana added. "Are we missing any clichés?"

"Yes. It prepares us for the future," Benny chimed in as he popped a dumpling into his mouth.

"Ruin our present is more like it," Gregory said as he climbed to his knees so he could reach the sauce on the table.

"These are so good, Mrs. Mercata!" Alex shouted out the dining room door.

"Thank you, Alex," came Mrs. Mercata's muffled reply from somewhere else in the house. "Now do your homework!"

"My parents," Benny whispered, "love that our time is filled with work. It makes them think we are learning more than we really are. I do not share this perception."

"I never even learn from homework," Gregory said as he put a selection of dumplings on a plate and sat down in a chair in front of his open math book.

"Math doesn't count, GK," Alex said. "Cuz you

don't learn it no matter what!" Alex grabbed two pencils and drummed a rimshot on the tabletop for emphasis. "Now let's get this show on the road! I'm leaving early, so I've got multiple hours of homework to do in ninety-seven minutes, people!"

"It's just gonna get worse, you know," Gregory said as he flipped the pages of his textbook. "Worse this year and worse every year after. By senior year we'll probably have twenty-five hours of homework a day."

"I am sooooo glad I met you, Gregory K. You are the sunshiny light to the dark of my black dresses." Ana laughed.

"You ain't seen nothing yet, Ana," Alex said. "Compare this to last year when he was getting ready for the citywide math tournament, and our friend Gregory is currently the king of comedy. Ooooh," Alex said in a fake imitation of Gregory's voice, "I'll nevvvverrrrr passssssss math. What can I do? Help me, Obi-Wan Kenobi! You're my only hope!"

Benny and Ana giggled, and even Gregory cracked a smile.

"Homework is not a variable, Gregory K.," Benny said with a shrug. "It is a constant, and you should use your energy to finish it, not to fight it. You'll be happier."

Gregory knew his friends were probably right about, well, about everything. But school was hard for him — he left a day of it exhausted and drained — and homework was harder. He even kind of liked school, really, or at least the best classes were enough to make the other classes tolerable. But it just all seemed off to him somehow. Like there was so much attention focused on knowledge he'd never need and skills he wouldn't use, and no time to develop the ones he felt would be important where his life would take him. Yet all around him adults told him that he would need those skills, he had to do these things, and he'd learn what was important later.

It didn't help that O and Kay had DNA that was designed for school. O had never met an assignment he couldn't fly through and get an A on while flying. Kay was only in fifth grade, but already she was taking online high school courses and still spending huge amounts of time playing with friends. They couldn't get enough schoolwork, and they thrived with all of it. Gregory was wired differently somehow, and this year, it wasn't a good somehow.

It wouldn't have bothered him so much except that here in middle school, it looked like everyone was simply doing "it" better than him, no matter what "it" was. He wasn't popular or getting great grades or being a star athlete or anything that he could figure out. Things like open mic night were what kept him going, what gave him hope. And now that was gone, and at the moment, nothing felt good.

Gregory couldn't focus on his homework at all, barely getting any done in the ninety minutes he worked on it. And when it came time for the group to switch to history homework, Gregory left his friends again and walked home. Kay was in the front yard Hula-Hooping when he arrived.

"Did you know that NASA studied Hula-Hoops? That makes what I'm doing rocket science, I figure," Kay said as her brother arrived.

"I thought you were actually taking a class in rocket science." Gregory put his backpack down and grabbed a Hula-Hoop from a small pile of them on the ground by Kay.

"Maybe next year. Right now I figure all work and no play would make Kay equal to O," his sister replied.

Gregory put the hoop around himself and gave it a

43

spin in the air. He quickly got into the rhythm as the hoop hit his hips, and he and Kay twirled their hoops together. Gregory wasn't an athlete, but this was something Kelly had taught him years ago and, like riding a bike, the skill didn't go away.

"Wanna do my homework for me?" Gregory asked his sister after a little bit. "I'll pay you or something."

"Oh, Gregory. I don't want your money, and I won't do your homework." Kay reached down and grabbed another hoop while keeping the first one spinning.

"It was worth a shot," Gregory said, hips wiggling. Kay held the second hoop like a Frisbee and gave it a spinning toss toward her brother. He leaned at just the right angle with his hands held high, and in a split second the second hoop joined the first one spinning around his waist.

"Dr. Bankster didn't bite your head off, I see," Kay said while grabbing another hoop for herself.

"No. He was pretty nice, actually. And Ana was in his room before me, which totally threw me," Gregory added, starting to get a little winded.

"Why was she there?" Kay asked.

"I was too busy trying to keep my heart from pounding through my chest, so I didn't ask her. Then

I forgot about it." Gregory said. "I'm sure it was about homework, though. Homework sucks. I wish it had never been invented."

"Write a poem about it," Kay suggested. "You'll feel better."

"Only if I can turn it in for credit." Gregory twirled the hoops up his body and back down again.

"Wow. That makes me hate homework too, if that's what you think about poetry now." Kay looked at her brother with concern. "I'm sorry."

"It's okay. Not your fault at all." Gregory grabbed one hoop and spun it the other way around him. He kept his hips moving and soon had the two hoops going in opposite directions.

"You can raise your grades, can't you?" Kay asked, genuinely concerned. Gregory gave her a thumbs-up. "Good. I hate you missing open mic night, but missing Elton Edwards . . ."

"That cannot happen!" Gregory shouted. "No. I will lie, cheat, steal, and beg before that happens. All of them at once if I have to."

"Or you could do your homework," Kay said.

"You really think I'm not trying?" Gregory asked as the hoops began to lose their rhythm.

"I know you are," Kay said. "I wish I knew the answer for you."

Gregory suddenly stopped twisting. The Hula-Hoops fell to the ground. " 'The answer is in history.' "

"What?" Kay also stopped twisting and stepped out of her fallen hoops.

"Nothing," Gregory said as he quickly unzipped his backpack and dug around inside. "Or maybe . . ." He pulled out Dr. Bankster's list of extra-credit assignments and skimmed it rapidly.

"Maybe what?" Kay asked as she joined her brother.

"Yes!" Gregory held up his hand, and he and Kay exchanged an awkward high five. "Yes! Yes! Yes! I'm gonna do some extra-credit homework!"

Kay watched as her brother zoomed into the house, chanting, "Homework! Homework! Homework!" Gregory knew he must sound and look bizarre, but he didn't care. It was homework time, and he had hope.

Inventor?
Tormentor!
Fated
To be hated.

As soon as dinner was done, Gregory plopped himself down at the computer he shared with Kay and got online. The computer was in the kitchen on a beat-up old desk in the corner. His parents didn't allow anyone to have a computer in their room—O's was up in the Lab, an office in the attic he shared with their father, and Gregory and Kay came to the best-smelling room in the house when they needed the Internet. And tonight, Gregory needed to do some research.

Dr. Bankster's extra-credit assignments weren't designed to be easy, and the bigger ones weren't designed to be done fast. The good news was that Gregory had figured out he only needed to raise his grade one point to get back to a C−, so he didn't have to pick a super-long project. The bad news was . . . well . . . that he had to do history homework at all. And that he only had three days to do it.

One of the choices on Dr. Bankster's list was to write a report about a person who'd had an impact on American history before the Revolutionary War and still had an impact today. The person couldn't be mentioned in the class textbook, and you had to reference at least two primary sources of research, write with footnotes, and probably do an interpretive dance too. Right now, Gregory wasn't concerned with any of that. He just wanted to know if there was a paper here to write at all.

It took a few different tries on Google, but suddenly, Gregory K. was grinning from ear to ear.

"Hello, Roberto Nevilis!" Gregory looked at his computer screen. "Don't take this personally, but I hate you."

Over the next hour, Gregory scoured the Internet, trying to find out what he could about Roberto Nevilis, a schoolmaster from Venice, Italy, who may, in fact, have been the inventor of homework back in the year 1095.

The sources online were sketchy — **Wikipedia didn't even mention the man (not that Dr. Bankster would let him use Wikipedia as a primary source anyway)** — but the fact that someone was named as the creator of the dreaded work was good enough for him.

The time frame of the late eleventh century was also satisfying. Last year, Gregory's school year had been saved by Leonardo Fibonacci, a mathematician who also lived in Italy hundreds and hundreds of years ago. What were the odds?

Gregory printed out a few documents, did a little research to make sure that kids actually went to school in the United States before the American Revolution, and then decided that he'd done enough for now. He could write a paper for Dr. Bankster and get a point on his average while making a point too. It was a win-win, and for a moment Gregory was actually grateful for Roberto Nevilis.

The moment passed quickly.

Excited that he had an idea that might just save him, Gregory turned off the computer, grabbed his printouts, and headed for his room. He had always kind of liked his basement hideaway, though he'd never really loved the final steps to it, down a long hall covered with O's and Kay's awards and honors, all framed on the wall. This summer, though, his dad had hung up a few framed copies of the Fibonacci poems Gregory had written for the City Math contest last year, as well as his certificate of participation. Somehow, the hall seemed friendlier now, even though none of his stuff said "Best" or "Outstanding" on it.

Once he got to his room, Gregory reached for his cell phone. He could only call a few numbers from it, but one of those was Kelly's, and tonight they were scheduled to talk. They mostly communicated by email since she'd moved away, something they figured made sense since they both loved to write. But there was no question in Gregory's mind that when he talked with Kelly, he felt calmer. And tonight was a good night for calm.

"You did what?" Kelly asked when he told her the details of his own personal tea party.

"You honestly said that?" Gregory asked when Kelly explained how she'd told off the captain of the track team when he'd suggested that girls shouldn't run cross-country.

The two told jokes and stories, Kelly read him a page from her book, and Gregory read her his poem about being grounded. Kelly told him how hard it was being the new kid in town, and Gregory told her about Ana trying to fit in with him and Alex and Benny. They probably would have talked all night, but their parents limited the calls to thirty minutes.

"You have to raise your grade, Gregory K.," Kelly said as the call was wrapping up. "You can do that report."

"I hope so. I really want to go to Booktastic on Friday," Gregory said.

"You can miss that, if you have to. It'd suck. But if you miss Elton Edwards"—Kelly's voice dropped to nearly a whisper—"I am never going to forgive you."

"No chance of that. I promise." As soon as he said it, Gregory regretted his choice of words.

"Calf!" Kelly shouted through the phone, and instantly his calf began to hurt as if she'd kicked him there. Kelly laughed as he groaned.

"What shoes are you wearing? That was so painful!" Gregory realized he was actually limping, even though nothing had touched him. "Anyway, I'll try hard. I promise that." The pain subsided, but Gregory still knew he was on dangerous ground. Not with Kelly, but with himself. It was still so easy for him to promise people what they wanted to hear, and Kelly was the best person ever at making him see what he was doing. Without her around, he always worried. "I wish you still lived here, Kelly."

"Me too, Gregory K. Me too."

When Gregory hung up a few seconds later, he went over to the far wall of his room — the wall that his father had painted over with blackboard paint years ago. In the past, his dad had left him math equations to solve, but this year, the board was his alone. Gregory found some chalk and wrote in big letters: "Work on history HOMEWORK!" It wasn't a note he ever thought he'd write for himself, but not much about seventh grade had gone as he'd expected anyway.

Bedtime came quickly, and Gregory put his notes carefully into his backpack. In the last moments before he turned off his lights, he read over his poems for open mic night. Optimism breeds good work, his mother always said, and nothing would show optimism more than believing he'd be at Booktastic Friday night.

He went to sleep and dreamed of poems chasing

homework papers. The poems won. That, Gregory figured, had to be a good omen.

The school day came and went, as inevitable as the tides. Gregory worked on his report during the lunch hour, slipping off to the school library rather than hanging with his friends. He found nothing else about Roberto Nevilis, but he did grab useful information about school in Colonial American times.

After school, Gregory walked with his homework crew to Alex's house and told them about his plan.

"You're doing homework about homework because you haven't been doing your homework," Benny said, trying to wrap his head around it.

"I guess you could look at it like that," Gregory admitted. "I'd rather just say I'm doing extra credit."

"Let me guess, dude. You're gonna do this extra credit instead of all your other homework," Alex said as he walked along, juggling three tennis balls.

"Unless you can give me the gift of time," Gregory said.

"Your birthday's not for a while, GK," Alex said, "and I don't have that type of money anyway."

"You really telling me that you can write a five-page paper by Friday morning?" Ana asked. She turned around and walked backward in front of Gregory so she could look him in the eye.

"The writing's not the problem," Gregory said.

"It's not poetry!" Alex added.

"Yeah, yeah. I write other stuff too, you know," Gregory replied. "And I've found this guy, Roberto Nevilis, who may have been the inventor of homework, and . . ."

"I hate him so bad," Ana interrupted and flipped around to forward walking again.

"If it hadn't been him, no doubt it would have been someone else," Benny said. "Don't waste your energy hating the dead. He is dead, isn't he?"

"Nine hundred years dead at least. My problem now is that I can't find good information on him. So, uh, I'm gonna head out to the library this afternoon," Gregory said. "Can you guys deal without me?"

"We'll call you if we need help on the math," Benny said good-naturedly.

"Five pages" was all Ana said, shaking her head.

"Best of luck, young Padawan," Alex said in his best Yoda voice. "And remember. There is no try. There is only do extra homework. Find multiple primary sources, may you."

"Nerd," Gregory said with a laugh as he peeled off from his friends.

"Geek!" Alex shouted after him. "Just like you!"

Gregory gave Alex two thumbs-up without turning back around. He was a man on a homework mission, and there was no more time to waste.

That night, and in every free minute the next day and night, Gregory researched and wrote, wrote and researched. He didn't get together with his friends to do homework, didn't study for his math quiz, didn't do his own writing, didn't do his daily reading, didn't practice his Spanish, and didn't sleep as much as he knew he should have. That would all have to wait. The paper was key.

For him, researching was always harder than writing. In the past, he would've tried to bluff his way through with his writing skills, but everyone knew that Dr. Bankster would throw an entire paper out if he detected shoddy research. Gregory didn't need to get an A on this extra credit, but he couldn't have a zero.

One big problem was that there was very little information available about Roberto Nevilis, who, unfortunately, was the person Gregory was writing about. Still, beyond Nevilis, the research was more interesting. It turned out that back in Colonial America, not every child went to school, particularly not older kids. School was for the wealthy, and college for the few. Kids did work outside of school all the time—chores, farming, family businesses—and that, more than academics, was their homework. Then there was the whole fighting for freedom thing that teen-agers ended up having to deal with, and homework didn't factor into that.

Gregory felt no need to dig into sources about whether Nevilis's invention was still having an impact today. Gregory was living proof—a witness to history, if he said so himself.

Friday morning, Gregory got up hours before normal to make sure he had time to finish typing and printing his report. His mom even made him her special French toast for breakfast.

"I am proud of you, Gregory," she said. "I'll check your grades with you after school, and I can still take you to Booktastic tonight."

Gregory gave his mom a hug. He knew that she'd turned down a movie night with friends to keep the evening free, even after he'd gotten the D. He was mad at her for having grounded him, of course, but he knew she cared. Not enough to let him go no matter what, of course, but Gregory figured that's what parents had to do.

At school, Gregory dropped off the paper during history class. Dr. Bankster told him to come by at the end of the day, and somehow Gregory managed to make it through his classes without falling asleep or exploding with anxiety.

Finally, the day ended, Gregory's friends wished him luck, and he headed toward the four flights of stairs that would lead him to learn his open mic fate.

As Gregory trudged up the steps to Dr. Bankster's room, he was pretty sure that the staircase had doubled in length since the morning . . . though he knew it was mostly the worry that after all his hard work, he'd still get the Red Pen of Bankster right through his heart.

When he arrived at the classroom, his teacher was sitting behind his desk, sipping tea. "May I offer you a cup, Gregory K.?" Dr. Bankster asked.

"No, thank you," Gregory replied. He had decided that accepting tea would somehow give his teacher the upper hand, so he'd vowed to say no whenever asked. He had to admit, though, the tea smelled great.

"Have a seat, please. I am finishing your paper now. It is . . ." The long pause made Gregory's neck hairs stand on end. "Inventive," his teacher finally finished.

Was that a good thing? Gregory wasn't sure and wasn't going to ask. He sat at the chair opposite Dr. Bankster and watched as his paper was read.

A few years ago, Gregory had had a terrible experience at the dentist when he discovered that the sound and feel of the dentist's drill made his skin crawl and his brain practically shake. Getting a filling in a baby tooth hadn't seemed like such a bad thing, and the laughing gas was no problem, but even now, years later, the mere thought of that drill made Gregory want to vomit. He had always thought it was the worst experience he'd face, but sitting here now watching Dr. Bankster scratching notes in red pen all over his paper was giving it a run for the money.

Every now and then, Dr. Bankster would grunt or say a soft "oh my," and rain red ink onto his paper. Once, his teacher laughed outright. "The word you wanted was *scholar*, not *schooler*, Gregory K. Perhaps you could use a little spelling homework?"

Gregory stayed quiet until his teacher finished. Finally, Dr. Bankster laid the paper on his desk and put his pen back in his pocket.

"Do you think Roberto Nevilis invented homework?" Dr. Bankster asked.

Gregory thought of a dozen different ways he could answer the question. He could redirect it, reframe it, lie, change the subject, or any other number of things. But he figured Dr. Bankster had seen it all before.

"I have no idea. He might not even be a real person. But someone invented homework, right? And it certainly has had an impact on American history," Gregory said as undefensively as possible.

"That is true. What is not true is that Patrick Henry said, 'Give me less homework or give me death.'" Dr. Bankster took a sip of tea without ever taking his eyes off Gregory.

"I said that was only a rumor," Gregory responded. "The truth is, there wasn't much to go on. You can look at my sources."

"There wasn't much to go on. Yes. True. Then why did you pick this topic, Gregory K.?" Dr. Bankster looked genuinely curious. "You must have learned early on that most colonists didn't send their children to school. You explained very well that homework could include chores, of course, but still. Your paper is more like historical fiction than history. So . . . why?"

"Because, to be honest, you seem to love homework and I thought you'd be interested to know that no one has ever been brave enough to take credit for its invention. Plus, I really liked my Patrick Henry quote." Gregory smiled as best he could. "I really worked hard, Dr. Bankster."

"Despite all the red ink I spilled, I am well aware that you did. And I do appreciate the hard work." Dr. Bankster reached into his desk drawer and pulled out his leather-bound grade book. "It is important to learn, however, that a good paper requires more than just hard work. It requires a legitimate subject, solid research, excellent grammar, and a convincing presentation. Is that clear?"

Gregory's heart sank as he nodded. Dr. Bankster reached into his pen pocket, but Gregory didn't even look.

"Good. I expect you to use that information if you do another paper. Hand in one like this again, and it won't help you." Dr. Bankster pulled the blue pen out of his pocket and flipped open the grade book. "But for your first effort, it's good enough."

"Oh! Thank you, Dr. Bankster!" Gregory said in complete shock. "And, um, well, are you going to enter that into the computer today?"

"The moment you leave, Gregory K., so that I may leave as well." Dr. Bankster flipped his grade book shut. "Have a good weekend."

Gregory leapt to his feet. "I will! Thank you, sir!" On the way downstairs, Gregory was convinced that someone had removed a few flights. Alex later told him that he'd been jumping down, skipping three steps at a time. Gregory didn't notice. He had to get home and get his poems ready. It was open mic night!

"Oh, come on, Mom!" Gregory said impatiently shortly after he got home, as his mother sat at the kitchen computer. "You just got that password!"

"Patience, Gregory," his mom replied. She pecked

at the keyboard again. "The ParentPortal site is very sensitive."

"So am I right now," Gregory said. "Can I type for you?"

"Somehow, I don't think it would be good if you knew my password here," Mom said with a smile. "Ahh, I'm in."

"I hope he updated it," Gregory said as he joined his mom in looking at the screen. "He said he would."

"History. Here we go." His mother clicked and they both waited. "Loading. Loading. Aha!"

"Look!" Gregory pointed to the big, shiny C– on screen.

"Good for you." His mother clicked the back button on the ParentPortal.

"I'm gonna go get my stuff," Gregory said as he started across the kitchen. "Can we go in, like, fifteen minutes?" His mother didn't answer. "Mom?"

Gregory turned back around. His mother was staring at the computer screen, and she didn't look so happy.

"Mom?" Gregory waited until his mother looked over at him.

"You should come see this," she said.

Gregory went back to the computer, totally confused. He had to get ready for open mic night, and his mom knew that. She was going to drive him, and she had to get ready too. Unless . . .

His mother pointed. Gregory looked. The computer showed his current grades, with first-period history a beautiful C−.

Math and Spanish, however, came next.

Both were now Ds.

4 Down I went on bended knees.
"Ignore," I said, "ignore the Ds.
I'm trying hard, so please,
please, please . . ."
It didn't work.
There's no good ending.
Move along. Nothing to see here.

"That's not possible!" Gregory exclaimed. "I had Cs!"

"C minuses," his mother clarified. "But you don't anymore. I'm sorry, Gregory."

"Mom! It's a mistake. I even got a seventy-four on the math quiz yesterday. It's got to be a mistake." Gregory looked at his mother pleadingly. She looked at the screen again.

"Well, let's see if we can figure it out." His mom clicked on the ParentPortal and looked at the new screen. But Gregory was one step ahead of her. He collapsed on the nearest chair.

"Homework," he said.

"Oh, Gregory. Did you really stop turning in your math?" His mother looked at him with equal parts sympathy and frustration.

"What's the point of turning it in when you haven't done it?" Gregory's shoulders slumped.

"Yes. Well. Perhaps I should've asked the question differently." His mother clicked around some more on the ParentPortal. "Spanish is the same thing."

"I was busy! There's just too much homework, Mom. Look at my test grades. Look at my papers! Homework is killing me, and that's not fair." Gregory tried his sad puppy dog eyes again. "Can we please go to Booktastic?"

For a moment, Gregory could see sadness in his mother's eyes, but then she gave him an even look. "No. A deal is a deal."

Sad and angry, Gregory retreated to his room, but even his notebooks and the smiling face of Albert Einstein on the giant poster on his wall didn't make much difference. He wasn't at open mic night, and he wasn't going to be there. He was missing something he loved, something that fulfilled him.

And it was his own fault.

Although really, when he thought about it while he

curled up on his bed with his pillow on top of him, that was only part of the story. Homework was the other part.

Gregory had always worked hard in school, even when he'd had crazy plans that led to some ill-advised stunts like tea parties, and this year was no exception. Sure, maybe he had taken some shortcuts in the past, and he didn't always do every single thing that was asked of him on every single assignment.

But the thing was, seventh grade was tough, and he really felt like he was learning this year. His test results showed it too. Homework, though. Well, that was a different story. Even with his group of friends, Gregory had struggled to get the work done. Sometimes he made excuses, sure, but most days . . . no. He just couldn't do it all. He didn't know how anyone could. He just . . .

Throwing off the pillow, Gregory walked over to his chalkboard wall, grabbed an eraser, and cleaned it off. He picked up a piece of chalk and wrote in big letters at the top of the board: HOMEWORK.

Ten minutes later, Gregory sat on the floor looking up at the list he'd scrawled on his wall:

AVERAGE TIME PER DAY
Reading: 30 minutes
(plus one minute to log)
Keyboarding practice: 15 minutes
Math: 30—60 minutes (takes Alex 10)
English: 20—25 minutes
(takes Ana 45—50)
Vocabulary: 5 minutes
Science: 20—30 minutes
(takes Benny 10—15)
Required science and math video lessons:
10 minutes 2x a week
History: 45 minutes

Although he wasn't good at math, Gregory could add those numbers up and see that homework for him could take three hours a day or longer, if he did it all. Then there were the big projects that got assigned, and while teachers would often drop some homework during the crunch time, the big projects always took longer than the daily work.

Three hours a day!

Now, he knew that Alex got his homework done

faster and would often get his reading done while the rest of the group finished math or science sheets. The keyboarding was something that Gregory felt he didn't need to do since he'd been typing since he was six, so maybe he shouldn't count that. And he also knew that sometimes, working in a group slowed things down a bit. On his own, he probably could do science in fifteen to twenty minutes rather than thirty, and he could shave time off on English most days, but with math? Well, without the presence of his friends, it'd take N minutes where N was very, very large. So he figured the time-with-friends thing was a net positive in terms of time, and certainly in terms of sanity.

Three hours a day!

Gregory stood up and started pacing. If he looked at each class separately, the load wasn't that bad. And if he looked at the work itself, it's not like it was over-whelmingly terrible. There was never a math sheet with fifty problems or anything, and the vocabulary words he could learn in about one minute. And they'd been good words, since Mr. Ahearn, his English teacher, was a writer, reader, and self-proclaimed crossword puzzle fanatic. And science was usually pretty fun, since they did a lot of experiments in class and the homework was often about them. And . . .

Three hours a day!

What if it took some kids a lot longer than it took him? What if they didn't have friends to work with? What if they had music lessons and the student paper and the speech team and basketball that they wanted to do or if they were learning to be a carpenter or volunteering at the animal shelter or trying to write a book that used to mean a lot to them but now seemed pointless?

Gregory's head was spinning, and he knew he had to get out of his room. He couldn't go to open mic night, but maybe his mom would at least let him have friends over so he didn't have to be alone and miserable. Still, one thing was for sure.

"I hate you, Roberto Nevilis!" Gregory shouted at his wall.

His mother agreed to let Gregory invite people over even though he couldn't go out. It was Friday night, however, and Alex and Benny were busy. But Ana was free and agreed to come on by even before Gregory mentioned that his mom was using her newfound free evening to bake a chocolate cake.

"That was delicious, Mrs. Korenstein-Jasperton," Ana said as she and Gregory sat at the dining room table picking the final crumbs off plates that once held chocolatey goodness.

"Thank you, Ana!" Gregory's mom beamed. She'd been baking frequently ever since Kelly and her mother had left town. Kelly's mom was the best baker ever, as far as Gregory was concerned. He used to eat her baked goods all the time at the Slice, the coffeehouse/bakery she used to run. This cake, he knew, was his mother's attempt to improve upon a recipe from the Slice. The cake was good, but it was definitely not an improvement. Gregory chose not to say anything, though, particularly since it was mighty fine cake . . . and there were leftovers.

"You're in a bad, bad mood," Ana said to Gregory once his mom had left with the dirty dishes. "That was great cake, and you haven't smiled."

"Did you know that we do three hours of homework every day?" Gregory asked.

"You do. It takes me longer. What's your point?" Ana twirled her hair absentmindedly.

"Do you know what we could do with that time?" Gregory stood up and began pacing around the table.

Ana shrugged. "But it's our job, ya know?"

"Why? Why is that our job?" Gregory's pace was fueled by anger and chocolate. "I don't get paid for it. Do you get paid for it? No. No one gets paid for it."

"My dad spends hours a day helping people for free. He says it's his job, cuz later other people hire him because everyone loves him and he's shown them he knows his stuff." Ana put her hand up in front of Gregory to stop him as he paced by. He gave her a high five instead and kept walking.

"And he gets paid in the end, and the end isn't ten years down the line. Homework is just all wrong. It's out of control!" Gregory zoomed around the table.

"So are you!" Ana grabbed Gregory's arm as he came past her again. "And you're making me dizzy."

"Sorry," Gregory said as he stopped. "I'm just angry about open mic night."

"Read me your poems." Ana said it simply, but it startled Gregory.

"What?" Gregory glanced over at her to see if she was serious. "Really?"

"You were gonna read 'em there, weren't you? So, now you get an audience of one girl who had nothing to do on a Friday night other than re-dye her blue hair." Ana grinned. "Seems like a deal to me."

"I dunno," Gregory said. "I'm just . . ."

The truth was that he'd never read or even shown his poems one-on-one to anybody other than Kelly or his teachers. Yes, he'd read them aloud in class and at open mic nights and at Author's Camp. Kay had seen some, but that didn't count because she'd read them first on her own and he only showed her the paper copies. This was new. And he barely knew Ana! With Kelly it was safe.

"Hey, it's no biggie," Ana said quickly. "We can just obsess over homework all night if you want. It's cool." Gregory could see she was a bit embarrassed, and that just made him feel terrible.

"You promise not to laugh at the poems, don't you?" Gregory said quietly. "I mean, unless they're funny ones!"

"I moved to town with one goal, Gregory K., and that was to make fun of you in every possible way. That's why I'm here tonight. I won't back down! Deal with it!" But Ana was laughing, and Gregory knew it was all going to be okay. Unless . . . No. He pushed that *unless* out of his mind. He would read, and it would be okay.

Gregory decided the best place to read the poems was in the living room, because there was a small area in front of the fireplace he could pretend was a stage. Ana sat on the couch, and Kay came in to join them, although Gregory wasn't sure whether that was because she wanted to hear his poetry or because she absolutely loved Ana's hair and earrings.

While he had only planned to read for the same seven and a half minutes he would've read at open mic night, Gregory added a few extra poems in the middle since his audience seemed engaged. He finished with the poem he called "My Best Friends."

"My best friends let me make mistakes.
They never, ever judge.
My best friends always help me laugh
and never hold a grudge.
My best friends never fight with me.
They have no gripes or whines.
My best friends make me stop and think
and read between the lines.

My best friends always comfort me.
They let me be outrageous.
My best friends are a quiet place,
a pen, and empty pages."

"Awesome," Ana said when the poem ended. "I've never been to something like this. Should I applaud?"

"I won't stop you," Gregory said with relief.

Ana leapt off the couch and clapped, stamped her feet, and whistled all at once. Kay gave a dainty golf clap.

"A fine performance, with echoes of early Silverstein and a dollop of Seuss," Kay said into an invisible microphone she pretended to hold. "The crowd was pleased, and Mr. Korenstein-Jasperton appears to be a young man to watch. Particularly because if not watched, he will try to take the dessert off your plate when you leave to go to the bathroom."

"Hey! That was three years ago!" Gregory laughed.

"It was apple pie. I will never forget," Kay replied.

"Thank you for sharing, Gregory K.," Ana said after stopping her ovation. "It was great."

Relaxed and pleased, Gregory smiled genuinely for the first time since the bad grade fiasco. "I was really nervous. A lot of those I'd never read aloud before either."

"I wish I could write like that," Ana said. "Poems or anything."

Kay looked at her and shook her head. "You're creative. I can tell. I bet you could write a great poem."

"If I could, nothing would stop me from writing, that's for sure." Ana's pocket buzzed and vibrated. She pulled out her cell phone to look at it. "My dad's on his way."

It was a beautiful early fall evening, and the moon and stars were bright enough to cast shadows on the street. Gregory and Ana went out to the porch to wait for her father.

"Thanks for coming over. I feel better." Gregory grinned. "And that's really all that matters, right?"

"Totally. That's really the reason I moved here," Ana said.

"Why did you move?" Gregory quickly followed on. "If that's okay to ask, I mean."

"Bunch of reasons, I guess. Mom got a job. A change of schools was sure good for me." Ana spotted a car heading down the street. "That's my dad."

"Kelly says she misses it here," Gregory said as Ana headed toward the street. "It must be hard to change."

"I don't miss a thing," Ana said. Her father's car

pulled up to the curb. "Thank your mom for the cake. And go write more poetry!"

Gregory waved good night to Ana and her father and decided that his new friend had a really good idea. Why let the night get him down—instead, since he had free time, he should use it to write.

Down in his room, Gregory carefully lifted the bottom of the Albert Einstein poster on his wall and opened the old fuse box behind it. Inside were all his notebooks full of writing. He grabbed a thick book of plain paper bound in a simple black cover and hurried over to his bed. On the floor nearby were a half-dozen discarded pencils, and he picked up the nearest one. He flipped the book open to the first blank page, put the pencil on the paper, and took a deep breath.

Many times in the past few years, Gregory had written this way until he fell asleep, often with the notebook still open. On good days, he'd get a draft of a poem or two done, rewrite older ones, or work on a short story. On really good days, he'd put the finishing touches on a piece and feel simply great. And tonight . . .

Tonight, every time he started writing, Gregory's eyes shifted over to his blackboard wall, where the homework list seemed to him to be staring right back, practically mocking him.

Since seventh grade had started, he'd barely written at all, other than for classwork, and it was homework's fault. School was important and all, but something about this year was really out of whack, and unless he put things back into balance, it wasn't going to get better.

Gregory popped out of his bed, once again working himself into a fast-paced pacing frenzy. If homework had already cost him open mic night—and he blamed homework, not his grades—what else would it do? Would it make him miss Elton Edwards? Would it stop him from writing at all? It would. He was convinced it would.

That wasn't okay.

There was a large bowl of chalk on the edge of Gregory's desk, and he rummaged through it until he found a big, thick stick of red chalk. He walked over to the homework list on the board, and in one smooth motion drew a giant circle around it.

Then, holding the chalk tight, Gregory drew a line through the circle at an angle, turning it into the universal "No" symbol.

He looked at his handiwork and felt good again.

No homework. That was a mantra he could live by. *Now*, he thought, *how do I make that happen?*

His calf started to hurt immediately after he thought it, and Gregory clutched his leg out of instinct. He limped back to his bed, dropping the chalk on his way. He curled back up with his poetry notebook, but his pencil sketched out a sign instead—homework with the "No" symbol through it.

Then, in small block lettering, he wrote a line from *The Lorax*: Unless someone like you cares a whole awful lot, nothing is going to get better. It's not.

He didn't know how he could make it better, but right now, Gregory was as determined as he'd ever been about anything. It all had to change, and he was the guy who would do it.

He hadn't a clue how, but that had never stopped him before.

"Roberto Nevilis," Gregory said as he closed his eyes, "you have met your match."

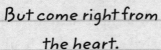

Some ideas arrive full form.
They're perfect from the start.
Some ideas take months
to cook,
But come right from
the heart.
Then there are the "ahhh!!!" ideas—
You blurt them out and . . . well . . .
They might be great or really bad
And only time will tell.

"You're talking weird again, dude," Alex said, tossing a Frisbee to Gregory across the Korenstein-Jaspertons' front lawn. It was early on Saturday morning, and the dew still sparkled on the grass.

"What is weird about wanting to change the home-work situation?" Gregory caught the Frisbee and tossed it back in one smooth move.

"Nothing. What's weird is that you think you can just go talk to the teachers and, boom, it'll change." Alex went for a between-the-legs catch, but coordination wasn't really his strongest suit. The Frisbee fell into the wet grass.

"Well, I'm open to ideas. That's why I called you . . ."

"And woke me up and didn't even offer me any chocolate cake." Alex grabbed the Frisbee from the ground and threw it super hard toward the street.

Gregory started to run after it until he saw Ana walking up the sidewalk, her boots clomping out a smooth rhythm. She adjusted her pace and angle to intercept the Frisbee's flight path, then reached out and popped it up in the air with a single finger on her right hand. The spinning disc went over her head and drifted to the other side of her body, where it was met by her left hand, which poked it back up and over to her right. She held up her right index finger and let the Frisbee land on it, spinning like a basketball.

"Nice throw," Ana yelled at Alex, then in one smooth move grabbed the disc and tossed back a strike.

"Whoa. You are awesome!" Alex shouted back happily.

"Dad plays Ultimate." Ana shrugged.

Benny pedaled up on his bike, wearing a helmet painted to look just like a watermelon. "I hear you have solved the homework situation, Gregory," Benny said as he hopped off his bike. "I am intrigued."

"Solved?" Alex laughed. "Solved? Dude, we're here today to do his homework about solving the homework situation!"

"Hey, I'll do this on my own," Gregory said, leading the foursome up to the house. "But seriously, are any of you happy with homework this year?"

"Like I said last night, Gregory K., it just is," Ana said.

"Then why did you come here this morning?" Benny asked.

"I didn't say I liked it," Ana replied.

The friends climbed up the three steps to the porch. Alex threw himself onto a rocking couch. Benny sat on a stool. Ana leaned against the railing, and Gregory paced.

"So, which class takes the most time for you?" Gregory asked. "For me, it's . . .

"Math," Gregory, Alex, Benny, and Ana said in unison.

"Right. No secret there," Gregory said. "Even with you guys, I can't get it all done in thirty minutes."

"English for me," Alex said, pumping his legs to get the couch moving.

"I'm not fond of Spanish," Benny offered. "And I speak the language to my grandmother."

"History," Ana said glumly.

"Oh yes," Benny said. "When I think about it, that's definitely where I spend the most time. It's just more interesting than Spanish, I guess."

"Right. Same," Alex added.

"So, look, it's different classes that are hardest for each of us, but even then, history wins the time war. And you know what?" Gregory asked. "Homework counts for one-third of our history grade! That's more than any other class. This is where we should start making changes."

"What is this 'we' you're speaking of?" Alex asked.

"You could talk to Dr. Bankster," Ana suggested.

"Or Principal Macallan," Benny added.

"Or the president of the United States! He could make changes." Alex put his feet down on the porch and stopped his swinging. "GK, I mean this nicely, but I don't understand your plan."

"Because I have no plan!" Gregory yelled back in frustration. "That's why you're here."

Ana strolled across the porch and sat down on the couch next to Alex. She pushed off the floor to get the couch rocking again.

"We're talking about trees and not seeing the forest," Ana said. "There's some bigger picture way to look at this."

"What do you mean?" Gregory asked. "Bigger than homework?"

"Bigger than each class in our school. Or bigger than each of us. Or something like that. But unless you're gonna go talk to every teacher and convince them to change their assignments . . ." Ana pumped her legs in unison with Alex.

"Unlikely to work, by the way," Benny added.

"Ya think?" Gregory replied.

"Dude, you can't be the first person to deal with this. I bet the answer is out there. Somewhere." Alex spun the Frisbee on his finger while the couch moved back and forth.

"Are you saying that the answer is in history?" Gregory was amused. "You and Bankster both."

"Yeah, well, sometimes teachers know what they're talking about," Ana said. "And unless you've got a better idea . . ."

Gregory didn't. He knew that. But doing research was an awful lot like doing homework, and that felt all sorts of wrong in light of the situation he was trying to address. He and his friends stayed on the porch for an hour more, talking, brainstorming, and laughing. And at the end of it all, Gregory knew that his only way forward was to do more work. Which sucked, really, but there was one upside: At least it wasn't math.

After his friends left, Gregory headed to the kitchen and waited for Kay to finish up on the computer. She had been teaching herself Latin for the past year and had found a Latin chat room to practice her skills. She'd been chatting for an hour already when her brother came in.

"I'll get off right now if you set the dinner table for me tonight," Kay said. "Quid pro quo."

Since he was grounded and certainly not going anywhere, Gregory took the deal.

As soon as Kay was done, Gregory slid in behind the computer and poised his fingers over the keyboard. What should he search for, he wondered? No more about Roberto Nevilis, an innocent figure if he was even real. After a moment, Gregory typed:

Why do we do homework?

He skimmed through the headlines the search engine brought back and clicked on a link or two, but there was nothing new here—it reinforces skills, it helps you learn time management, all the common answers he'd heard since he was young. He typed again:

How much homework should kids have to do each day?

This was more interesting reading, although answers were all over the place for all sorts of different reasons. One common guideline that came up a lot was ten minutes per grade level. This was easy math where Gregory saw a problem right away— seventy minutes compared to the one hundred eighty he was currently spending. But as he read more, it was clear that figuring out what ten minutes of homework looked like was tricky. Ten math problems took Alex two minutes and Gregory two hours, and that was the problem teachers had across the world.

Then there were the people who felt that reading shouldn't count as homework time and some people who thought you shouldn't require reading at all because that takes the joy out of it. He even read about a school where all the homework was watching video lessons, and then you did all the work sheets and problems in school instead of at home! Other countries had different ideas too, going from many hours a day to next to nothing.

In other words, Gregory thought, no matter what he said to his teachers, they could tell him what they were doing was okay. And maybe they were right from their perspective, but they sure weren't from his. It all seemed unfair in the extreme. Frustrated, Gregory typed once more:

Why is homework even legal???

When he explained it to his friends later, he said that twenty minutes passed as the computer thought and thought, and after all that time the only thing that appeared on his screen were the words *IT'S NOT, GREGORY K.* Neither part of that was true, of course, but it made a good story.

The truth was that a lot of links came back that led him to all sorts of angry fellow students asking the same question. Just as he was about to give up, he clicked one final link to what looked like a scholarly article published by a legitimate publication talking about homework and the law.

And while it wasn't quite *IT'S NOT*, it was certainly interesting:

In 1901, the state of California had passed a law abolishing homework for all children under the age of fifteen because, and this was Gregory's favorite part, it was agreed that homework was harmful to children. Other communities around the country had passed similar laws too, all agreeing that homework wasn't beneficial.

Exactly! Gregory thought. *Homework should be against the law. And it was!*

The early 1900s, Gregory discovered, was a period of great homework battles across the country, with folks arguing about the same questions people were still fighting about today. Was homework helpful? How much was too much? Shouldn't kids be home playing and doing chores when they weren't in school? Well, no, Gregory thought. Not just doing chores. But home doing other things they wanted . . . doing productive things that led them to a richer life? Yes, of course.

Unfortunately, the tide had turned again, and in 1917, California repealed the homework ban. Over time, the article said, schools everywhere reinstituted homework and the laws were forgotten. Battles moved to other things, though the homework arguments continued to the present day.

Well, homework had been illegal, anyway. That was something. On a whim, Gregory tried one more search — his hometown:

Homework law in Franklinville

Jackpot! There it was in 1901, a newspaper article about a city law the same as the California law!

A few years ago, Gregory had gone through a period of reading books about silly laws, such as people not being allowed to eat peanuts in church, or drivers having to pull their cars to the shoulder and cover them with a tarp if they approached a horse on the road. A lot of the laws made sense at the time, though now most of them just seemed odd, unimportant, or nonsensical. But the most interesting thing to Gregory was that a lot of the laws were actually still on the books. People had forgotten about them and never took action to repeal them. So, Gregory searched again:

Homework law in Franklinville repealed

Nothing came back. It wasn't conclusive, of course, and Gregory knew it. Still, there was a chance that homework was completely illegal in his town. And that . . . well . . . that was worth more research.

Monday after school, with his parents' permission, Gregory headed straight to the city offices in downtown Franklinville, an easy ten-minute walk from Morris Champlin. Alex joined him, but Ana and Benny decided to stick to their homework group schedule.

"But seriously, Gregory K.," Ana said as they parted ways, "I am wishing you the best of luck!"

The city clerk, Eleanor Stern, had worked at the town library with Alex's mother for years, and she didn't even bat an eye when the two boys told her they wanted to look through the city records to see if a law from 1901 was still on the books.

"You know how to use microfilm, don't you?" was all she asked. Alex nodded. "Good. Films are by decade. Records of the town council meetings. Look under 'actions taken.'"

Eleanor Stern led the boys to a dusty records room, fired up an old microfilm reader, and pointed them to a nearby shelf with rolls of film. "If you don't put these back in order, you will make me cry. And you don't want that, do you?"

After the boys were alone, Gregory turned to his friend and mused, "How are we supposed to answer that? Yes, we do? Rhetorical questions are weird."

"Focus, dude," Alex said. "This is gonna be sucky enough without talking English language stuff."

Gregory looked over at the shelf and found the film labeled 1901–1910. He grabbed the film container and handed it to Alex. "We need popcorn to make this the full movie experience."

"You can go ask Ms. Stern if you want, but I'm thinking it's a dead end," Alex said as he put the first film in the reader. "Okay, let's get to work."

Right away, the two boys found the original home-work law. Alex pressed a few buttons, and a printed photocopy of it spit out of the side of the microfilm machine.

"This is worth framing," Gregory said. He read from the paper. " 'Be it noted that the council finds homework to be detrimental to the health and welfare of growing children.' "

"People were so much smarter back then, weren't

they?" Alex asked. "I mean, they hadn't invented TV or the Internet yet, and movies were silent and people died from all sorts of horrible diseases all the time, but they got this one right!"

Gregory laughed. "Let's keep looking. And let's hope we don't find anything else. Ever."

The process was as boring as could be, although it wasn't that hard. One advantage of living in a small town was that not too many actions were taken by the city council over the course of a year, or even a decade. It didn't hurt that the council only met monthly either.

As they moved through the decades, they spoke less and less. It wasn't because they didn't have anything to say. Instead it was because they were now through the 1940s and the "no homework" law was still on the books. Saying something seemed like a jinx.

Eleanor Stern came in to give them the fifteen-minute warning as the boys scrolled through the 1950s.

"I almost want to stop now," Gregory said. "At least we'd feel good overnight."

"If this law still exists, do you think we can get teachers arrested or something?" Alex asked.

"Principal Macallan first. Gotta start at the top," Gregory replied. "Should we call it a day?"

"One more decade," Alex said, and both boys got back to the annoying job at hand.

The years 1961, '62, '63, and '64 seemed to zoom past . . . and the law was still on the books. Then came November of 1965, and both boys sagged.

"One more decade, you said," Gregory grumbled.

"Dude, you knew it was too good to be true," Alex said as he clicked buttons on the machine, printing out a new page.

"Why would they repeal that law all of a sudden in 1965?" Gregory wondered aloud. "It had been sitting there for over sixty years. Why did they suddenly remember?"

Alex scrolled the microfilm back a little bit. "Maybe the meeting notes tell all," he said. Gregory leaned over his friend to read the screen too.

"No. Way," Gregory said.

"It couldn't be, could it?" Alex asked.

Gregory read aloud, " 'In regards to a complaint filed by Roger Bankster, a minor residing in Franklinville, the mayor proposed repealing city code 3.1.7 Article C.

The council voted unanimously in agreement with the mayor."

"It figures," Alex said.

"Dr. Roger Bankster has always been out to get us," Gregory groaned. "Even before we were born!"

It had been a long shot, Gregory knew, but he was pretty bummed anyway. Imagine a law that protected him and all his friends from homework! It would've been great.

That night, he lay in his bed finishing up his math homework and silently cursing his history teacher. He went to sleep angry and woke up angrier. There was only one thing to do — even if it meant he'd fail later, he had to go to Dr. Bankster's office hours one more time.

Once again, Gregory found himself climbing up the stairs to Dr. Bankster's room early on a Tuesday morning. And once again, right as he climbed up the last flight of stairs, Ana came walking down, her blue hair and backpack bouncing in sync as she walked toward him.

"Morning, GK," Ana said.

"What are you doing here? I mean . . . like . . . why are you here?" Gregory paused. "That's kind of the same thing, isn't it?"

"I have to pick stuff up from Dr. Bankster." Ana didn't really slow down, so Gregory stepped aside to let her go past. "It's not a big deal, okay?"

"Yeah. Fine." Gregory watched her go. "I was just asking, that's all!"

Ana didn't reply, so Gregory refocused himself and climbed the last stairs to the office. He knocked and entered.

"Gregory K.," Dr. Bankster said from behind his desk, "to what do I owe the pleasure of your visit?"

"Homework," Gregory said, crossing the room. "You love it, and I don't. I'm tired of it. I need a break. We all need a break. But it seems like you've been on a homework kick for a long, long time."

Reaching into his backpack, Gregory pulled out a microfilm printout, sliding it over to his teacher. Dr. Bankster looked it over and let out a long whistle.

"It was 1965, was it? I'll be. Such a different period of my life." Dr. Bankster slid the paper back to Gregory.

"But yes, I have been interested in homework for many years."

"Why do you give us so much work, Dr. Bankster? Seriously, I'm not trying to be disrespectful, but I don't understand." Gregory waited for a response, standing tensely next to his teacher's desk. Dr. Bankster took a long sip of tea.

"There are many ways I could answer this question, Gregory K. But I'm an old man, and I've done this for a long time now, so I am going to put this simply in a way I hope you understand. You are like the early colonists. And I am like the King." Gregory waited for more, but Dr. Bankster simply sipped his tea, looking completely unconcerned.

"That's it?" Gregory's frustration was showing. This was not going the way he had hoped. "I thought maybe I could talk about how much time I work on your class, sir. I thought you'd listen."

"You can talk about it, but simply know that everything I say and every piece of work I assign is given for a reason. You might not like the reason. You might not understand the reason. You might think the reason is totally wrong. But that places you in a difficult position, since I know you want to pass my class. This means it's all up to you. You have choices to make, Gregory. I do hope you choose wisely." Dr. Bankster smiled up at Gregory. "Anything else?"

While there was a lot that Gregory wanted to say, he didn't even need Kelly to kick his calf as a warning—he knew he had to walk away. If this was a fight, he'd lost this round . . . and if he stayed longer, he'd never live to fight another day.

The homework crew gathered in the dining room at Gregory's house after school, filling the table with textbooks and homework packets and work sheets as they organized for the work ahead.

"Can we do science first?" Benny asked. "Then math, English, and history."

"Sure," said Alex.

"Fine," said Ana.

"Look at all this," said Gregory. He held up a sheaf of papers. "We have no rights. We're like early colonists, people. And our teachers are kings."

"And queens," Ana added.

"I want to write poetry today," Gregory said. "And I want to read a book for myself."

"And I want to fly to Hollywood and meet Darth Vader. What's your point?" Alex asked, neatening his piles.

"My point is that it doesn't have to be like this," Gregory said.

"It largely does," Benny replied quietly.

"No. I mean, seriously, we've all given up stuff because of this. Lots of stuff we liked, even if you pretend it's just cuz you're busy with other things, Alex. And people keep telling us we don't have a choice. We don't have power, right? But that's what they said to the colonists and to all sorts of other people all through history. It's just not true," Gregory said, standing up and waving his pile of papers. "We do have power. We just have to grab it."

"And how do we do that, GK?" Ana asked.

"Fail all our classes so we can bother our teachers until they give up?" Alex grinned.

"This is pointless, Gregory K. You're fighting the school. And parents," Benny said kindly. "We can discuss it over the weekend, but it's eating into our time now. Let's start our homework."

Benny, Alex, and Ana pulled out their science books, but Gregory didn't move.

"No. No more homework."

Gregory tossed his handful of papers into the air. While he hoped they'd spread out dramatically, they simply fell with a thump on the dining room table. Still, it was a solid thump.

"Dude, what do you mean?" Alex asked. "You quitting school?"

"Nope. I'm on strike." Gregory sat down triumphantly. "I am on a total, complete homework strike."

I remember when there was time to play,
When I could laze the day away.
Was that a dream?
 Or . . . wait. Oh, bummer.
That was what we call
"the summer."

Feeling totally triumphant, Gregory looked at his three friends expectantly, sure they'd see his brilliant idea and cheer him on, maybe even join forces with him.

"I don't get it," Benny said.

"You're out of your mind," Ana added.

Alex said nothing. Instead, he got up from the table, walked over to Gregory, looked him in the eye . . . then kicked his friend in the calf.

"Don't you see?" Gregory held up the homework again. "We can do what the colonists did. What people do all the time. We can insist on a change to unfair conditions."

"And we can fail all our classes," Ana said, shaking her head. "And when I say 'we,' I mean 'YOU.'"

"Yeah, yeah. There are always consequences," Gregory said. "But as Patrick Henry said, 'Give me liberty, or give me death!'"

Gregory looked at his friends, all of whom still seemed underwhelmed. "That was supposed to be my big convincing line there, you know," he said.

"Needs work," Ana replied.

"Look," Gregory tried again, "nothing's gonna change unless someone tries something new. I mean, kids like us have been complaining about homework for years, and nothing's changed. So I'm trying something else. Maybe you don't mind the homework, but I have stuff I want to do, and I can't do it. And I think it's important, and I'm tired of adults telling me I'm wrong."

"How does the strike work?" Benny spread his homework out across the table. "Just math? Just history?"

"Everything. Even if Dr. B. stopped assigning homework, we'd still have too much and the problem wouldn't be solved." Gregory began folding one of his pieces of homework. "I'm tired of everyone telling us what to do without asking us what we think or want."

"Like any child would say 'give us homework'?" Benny leaned back in his chair. "I'm sorry, I'm not following."

"We're not powerless, that's what I mean. It's our life. Shouldn't we have a choice?" Gregory folded again and again, making crisp lines as he went.

"You should spend more time with my parents," Benny said softly. "They would tell you no."

"We do have a choice." Ana looked directly at Gregory. "We can choose to pass our classes or throw away a year."

"I don't have a clue what you're really saying yet, GK," Alex said as he returned to his seat, "but I support your right to say it. Now, uh, I have to do my math homework."

"You do that. I'm gonna write some poetry," Gregory said as he made a final fold and held up a perfect paper airplane. "And I'm telling you, this strike is gonna fly."

With a smooth motion, Gregory tossed the airplane. It flew forward ten feet, slammed into the dining room wall, and tumbled to the floor. Ana tried to suppress a laugh, but she failed, and soon all four of the friends were laughing, though Gregory's laughter was not nearly as loud as the others.

"I got more writing done today than any day since school started." Gregory lay on his bedroom floor talking to Kelly on the phone. "Tell me that's not awesome."

"It's awesome," Kelly replied. "I'm baking."

Gregory sat bolt upright. "First of all, if it's apple pie, you're sending it to me. Second of all, how do you have time? Don't you have homework?"

"It is chocolate pie, and it's for school, so it's mine. And I got all my homework done, Mr. I Wrote More Today Than Ever." Kelly was briefly drowned out by a mixer or food processor, Gregory couldn't be sure. But it sounded like dessert, so he didn't care. "Be honest, since I'll know anyway. Did you get your math done or did you just skip it to write?"

This was the moment of truth, and Gregory squirmed where he sat. It was one thing telling the homework crew his plan. It was another telling Kelly. On the one hand, he knew he couldn't lie to her. She'd figure it out or find out, and then what? But on the other, he wasn't really looking forward to her response.

"I went on strike," he mumbled.

"What?" Kelly punctuated the question with the sound of a spoon clinking against a bowl. "Did you say you don't like something?"

"I said I went on strike. A homework strike." Gregory relaxed when the words were out. And then he waited. All the baking sounds had disappeared.

"That's interesting." Kelly paused a long time. "Talk me through it."

Standing up, Gregory realized that his calf was not hurting. This had to be a positive sign. Feeling emboldened, he explained the three-hours-a-day problem, the bad meeting with Dr. Bankster, and how he hadn't written all year. "So, I'm just not doing it anymore."

"What are your demands?" Kelly clinked and stirred. "You have to have demands or it's giving up, not going on strike."

"I dunno yet. It's . . . I mean . . . I want my time back. I don't want everyone telling me I have to do all this stuff when I don't see how it's important." Gregory stopped at his blackboard wall and stared at the homework chart. "I'd like homework to be different."

"That's not a demand," Kelly said before Gregory heard a kind of moist and grunty sound.

"You licked the beater!" he said with great familiarity.

"I did. And you didn't give me a specific action you want people to be taking to get you to end your strike. Reach for the moon, Gregory K. Don't go on strike for nothing." Kelly licked the other beater as Gregory thought.

"Maybe I should get the old law back. Make homework illegal again."

"Now that's a demand!" Kelly seemed satisfied. "Break it down now. What are the steps to get there? Do you go straight to Congress? The city council? Or do you have to start at the school level?"

"I have no idea, Kelly," Gregory admitted. "Probably start at the school? Yeah. School. But first, I have to start with me."

"And what do your parents say about all this?" Kelly asked.

For a second, Gregory thought about hanging up rather than answering. Instead, he did neither. He didn't need to. It was Kelly on the phone. He counted backward in his head: *three, two, one.*

"You haven't told them," Kelly said on cue. "Right. I forgot who I was on the phone with."

Kelly didn't say it with anger or dismissal, but Gregory felt it right in the heart. She continued, "I don't know if you know this, Gregory K., but your grades are gonna be in a world of trouble if you stop doing homework. And what if doing homework actually was teaching you enough that that's why you were doing well in your classes this year? And . . ."

Gregory interrupted. "Oh, come on. We all know I stink at school. O and Kay are the brains here."

"Do NOT ever say that again" — Kelly's tone meant business — "or there are no pies in your future."

"Whoa! Not fair!" Gregory was smiling, though.

"You do stink at school, but, Gregory K., your brain is one of a kind. If anyone can pull off a homework strike, it's you." Kelly inhaled loudly through her nose. "Hey . . . can you smell that?"

"You know I can." Gregory closed his eyes. Kelly was baking one of her mom's recipes, and he could call up that smell in a heartbeat. It was a happy smell. Not as happy as the apple pie smell, sure, but still perhaps the second-happiest smell in the world. "You think this is a good idea?"

"It's a you idea," Kelly said quietly.

What that meant wasn't clear, really, but Gregory figured it wasn't totally bad news.

It was a simple thing to skip one day of homework. Gregory had done that before, then worked his butt off to make up the work. It wasn't such a hard thing to tell his friends a crazy idea. He'd done that lots of times, and often backtracked the very next day. It was a totally different thing, however, to stick with an idea through thick and thin and deal with the consequences. That was something Gregory was not an expert at.

In truth, part of him expected that he'd wake up in the morning, do his English homework super fast, write something on science, then spill syrup on math and forget the idea had ever happened. After all, Ana's voice was stuck in his head — he was going to fail, and that wasn't a good outcome at all.

As it turned out, three things happened that changed his morning entirely. The first was simple: It was cereal day and there was no syrup to be found, so one option was gone. The second thing was totally unexpected, and happened when he, O, and Kay were having breakfast at the table and their mother came to say good-bye before she went to work.

"Your father and I talked it over, Gregory K." His mother was always cheery in the morning once she'd had her cup of coffee, and today was no exception. "It's a new quarter at school, and we want you to show us what you're all about. We know you'll get your grades up, and we know you don't want to spend all your time stuck at home. You're no longer grounded, and we won't look at your grades for four weeks."

"I love you" was all Gregory could think of saying. He meant it, of course, but it seemed incomplete. Still, it was better than "you are going to be SO sorry about that!"

"Suckers" was probably not all O could think of saying, but it was all he did say.

"That's just so sweet," Gregory said. "Tell him, Mom. Tell him how nice that was."

"Everyone is entitled to their own opinion. I choose to think that Owen is wrong. It wouldn't be the first time. Not even the first time this year," his mother said, then kissed each of her three children good-bye. "Have a good day, everyone. Make us proud!"

The siblings watched their mother go. O shook his head.

"You are so lucky," O said to Gregory. "If they watched your grades, you'd be grounded until the end of seventh grade!"

"Probably longer," Gregory agreed.

And it was then that the third thing happened.

"Grades are ridiculous," Kay said. "I got a 'needs improvement' on working and playing well with others last year. I was taking a college class and making friends with twenty-one-year-olds. I'd rather watch Gregory do something interesting than watch your report cards come in, O. Though I'd look at any of your math tests in a heartbeat!"

For a brief and rare moment, O was silent. Kay had that way about her, and Gregory figured it was her small size and big brain. Still, she could somehow make both him and O feel good about themselves at the same time, a skill even his mom and dad were lacking. And right now, Gregory was feeling good, because maybe he was doing something interesting and maybe people would want to watch, just like Kay said.

And maybe if enough people watched, it would be easier to make changes? A guy could dream, anyway.

For now, at least, it was enough to get him to school for strike, day one.

"So, dude," Alex said as he joined Gregory on the walk up the hill to school. "Did you do your homework late last night anyway?"

"Nope. I'm on strike." Gregory liked saying it. Speaking the words made it feel more real.

"Do you think anyone will know?" Alex turned around and walked up the hill backward next to Gregory. "I mean, don't get mad and say I'm being all O-like, but aren't teachers used to you not turning in homework?"

"This is none, though, not just partially done. I think that's new." Gregory thought it over. "I'll tell 'em at some point. I just want to enjoy a little freedom, you know? Get used to what I'm fighting for."

"Fighting? That word . . . I do not think it means what you think it means." Alex's long legs let him keep pace with Gregory up the steep hill. "You really didn't think this through, did you, dude?"

"Not at all," Gregory agreed. "But one day in, and I'm pretty happy."

As the week progressed, Gregory noticed, he felt better and better. He still got together with his friends every day during homework time, but as they did work for school, he worked on his own things—most days writing poems, some days writing short stories, and once even doing absolutely nothing at all. It felt fantastic. Every now and then he'd help Ana or Benny with English, and sometimes he joined in on talk about science class experiments or the history lesson itself, but he never once laid pencil to homework paper.

His friends didn't know what to make of the new Gregory. Ana asked and almost begged him to get back to doing his work "for his own good." Benny occasionally said, "I do not understand you" out of nowhere. And Alex started calling him "Gregory F.," but he always laughed, so it didn't seem too harsh.

At school, nothing had changed either. That was probably both good and bad, Gregory realized, and probably for the same reason. So far, he hadn't told anyone besides his friends that he was on strike. He simply wasn't turning in his homework. He came to class every day and participated like normal, so he figured no one was noticing anything. This was great because he felt happy and free when he was skipping homework. But he had to agree with the trio of friends when they suggested that, well, he was not getting closer to his goal of change.

But it felt good! For the first time since seventh grade started, Gregory was happy again.

Until Friday. That was the day that Dr. Bankster asked to see him after school. At lunch that day, Gregory sat with Alex, Ana, and Benny. And he was nervous.

"You're so busted, dude," Alex said. "You knew it would be Dr. B., didn't you?"

Gregory nodded. He took a bite of his sandwich and his day got worse. "Ugh. Weird Wednesday dinner is bad enough," Gregory said, referring to the night his mother always tried new recipes. "But giving it to me as leftovers on Friday is cruel."

He showed his sandwich to his friends. They cringed in order.

"Is that alive?" Ana asked.

"No. It's tofughetti in brown sauce on gluten-free bread that failed to rise." Gregory took another bite. "I took it for lunch in exchange for O giving me his bacon this morning. Actually, not a bad trade."

"If you don't mind my saying, Gregory K., this would be a good time to cease your strike," Benny said very seriously. "Dr. Bankster calling you in is your worst-case scenario."

Ana shook her head. "Disagree. Whatever it is you're expecting, I think you'll be surprised."

This was good news to Gregory because he was expecting a scolding, a call to his parents, and a firing squad . . . and he was kinda hoping the order would be reversed. He was still expecting the worst as he climbed the stairs after school and entered the history classroom.

With his teacup raised, Dr. Bankster ushered Gregory over to the desk, where he sat surrounded by piles of paper. "Cup of tea for you?"

"No, thank you, Dr. Bankster." Gregory sat nervously opposite his teacher.

"I am grading homework, Mr. Korenstein-Jasperton. And once again, I have none from you. Would you care to tell me why?" Dr. Bankster asked pleasantly, but Gregory noticed that his red pen and grade book were on top of his desk — a silent threat.

It would have been easy for Gregory to make up an excuse or feign surprise. But as he thought of those options, his calf began to hurt spontaneously. So he took a deep breath, looked his teacher in the eye, and said, "I'm on strike, Dr. Bankster. A homework strike."

Dr. Bankster sipped his tea calmly. Whatever reaction Gregory had expected, it wasn't this. This was no reaction at all. After a long pause, the teacher put down his tea and leaned toward Gregory.

"What are you on strike for?" Dr. Bankster asked, his eyes sparkling.

"Um . . . no more homework," Gregory said quietly.

"No more homework? Teachers just stop?" Dr. Bankster shook his head. "How does that happen?"

"That law that made homework illegal? I want it back," Gregory said.

"Interesting," Dr. Bankster said with a nod. "Does your strike need to spread, or can you do it alone? How will you let everyone know what you stand for? What is the process by which a strike leads to a change in the law?"

"Uh . . ." Gregory was taken aback by the intensity in Dr. Bankster's voice.

"Young man, a strike is a powerful thing. It is not something to be undertaken on a whim or because you want a week off homework. You must be prepared for serious challenges and serious consequences." Dr. Bankster rose from his seat. "Are you?"

"So far the only consequence is that I'm happier," Gregory said.

"No!" Dr. Bankster pounded on his desk. "Another consequence is that your grade in my class, and I assume every other class, is falling. That is a serious consequence, Gregory K., and if it is going to happen because of an action you are taking, you better make that action count for something. So why a strike?"

"I feel powerless," Gregory said. "Being a kid . . . it's like we're the end of the road. No one cares. Everyone has power over us."

"Are you saying that down at the bottom you, too, should have rights?" Eyes twinkling, Dr. Bankster walked over to a closet behind his desk and unlocked it. "Wait there, please," he said as he disappeared inside.

Stories about Bankster's closet were many. Some said Dr. Bankster had kept every paper every student had ever written for him inside it. Other people were convinced it was full of red pens so that he'd never run out. O claimed it was full of the same type of cheap prizes you got at the dentist's office for sitting through a cleaning when you were a kid, but the idea of Dr. Bankster and whoopee cushions was one that didn't work for Gregory. This was a mystery he'd love to solve, but Dr. Bankster had closed the door behind himself. Gregory could hear rustling inside and sat wondering what terrible fate would befall him.

Before terribly long, Dr. Bankster emerged carrying a pile of books. This was a bit of a disappointment, really, as the stories of the closet held so much potential. Books, while wonderful things, weren't really mysterious.

One by one, Dr. Bankster laid the books in front of Gregory, giving bullet-point narration as he went. "Chapter seventeen, the Pullman strike. In this one, chapter eight, the steel strike of 1919. Do not confuse it with the steel strike of 1959."

"Uh . . . of course not," Gregory said.

"This one talks of the postal worker strikes. You'll find the pages marked. This one looks like a picture book, I know, but it's a good summation of the newsboy strike of 1899. That one is particularly relevant, Gregory K., because it was youth against the establishment. Here is a fabulous story about the Boston Tea

Party, something I know you're familiar with. It's not a strike, of course, but if you think you're going to lead the charge to change, it is important to read." And on Dr. Bankster went through eight books. "Finally, here is *Click, Clack, Moo* in case you've forgotten what the point of going on strike is."

"I don't understand," Gregory said. "Why are you giving me these?"

"Because there is an important corollary we don't mention often. We say that if you don't know history, you are doomed to repeat it. The corollary is that if you do know history, there are parts that you might very well want to repeat." Dr. Bankster opened his bottom desk drawer. "One final book, but you must promise to take care of it."

The moment it came out, Gregory recognized it. "*Yertle the Turtle*! I knew that 'down at the bottom' line sounded familiar."

"It will teach you a lot, Gregory K., if you think about it." Dr. Bankster neatened the pile of books. "I suggest you read these over the weekend or give up your strike today. The choice is yours, of course. But do understand: Right now your strike is pointless, and I will crush you without doing anything. We all will."

Almost by instinct, Gregory grabbed the pile of books. He stood up, said his good-byes, and was half-way down the flight of stairs before he realized what had happened.

"I have homework!" he said aloud. It echoed around the staircase. Somehow, though, this work seemed worth doing. In his head, he rearranged his weekend plans. The strike was something he wanted to do, so despite it all, he knew the truth: It was time to get to work.

It can't be overstated:
Planning's underrated.

7

It was a truly unexpected turn of events, Gregory thought as he looked at the pile of reading Dr. Bankster had given him. At first he figured he'd skim quickly through one or two of the books or just read the Seuss and tell his teacher he'd done more. But once he started reading, he got sucked in.

Strikes, it turned out, were really interesting. Scary too. He read about strikers losing jobs and friends. He read about people getting "roughed up" by henchmen hired by one side or the other. He read about imprisonment and death, and strikes that worked and strikes that didn't.

As he read, a major truth became clear: If he was going to succeed, he was going to need allies. Lots of them. Being on strike by himself didn't give him any leverage at all. The only thing it did was put him at risk. No teacher or school was going to engage in the conversation about change if it was only him speaking softly on the other side. But being a leader of a cause with people following him was way different than making a quiet statement.

Some of the pictures in the books were certainly inspiring, though. Throngs of people holding banners and signs demanding better treatment. And really, wasn't that what Gregory was seeking? Like the colonists and newsboys before him, Gregory was demanding freedom from the tyranny of rich or powerful overlords!

He'd just ignore the pictures of the penniless, broken, and bloodied.

All weekend, Gregory read about what had happened in the past. About the great voices and leaders and the challenges people making change had faced. By Sunday night, he was wavering. He still had time to get back to work with no one but his friends knowing he'd failed in his mission, and his friends certainly wouldn't care. Heck, they didn't even think it was a mission yet. So far, it was just a week of skipping homework.

At breakfast Monday, Gregory was so lost in thought that he almost missed out on the bacon his mom brought to the table and had to make a last-minute deal with O to snag some.

"I know that look in your eye," Kay said to Gregory when breakfast was done. "And just for the record, I'm excited."

"That makes one of us," Gregory replied. He headed off to school, glad to have the day to really think things through. By watching what went on in class with this new perspective, he figured he'd get to see if his efforts made sense and had a chance to work. Otherwise, he'd close it down and move on.

Monday was always tough, since the start of any week at school was more challenging than the end, at least for Gregory. Even being on strike and not having done homework all weekend didn't change that. He and Alex trudged up the stairs to history class together, as happy as Monday would allow.

In class, students took their seats and pulled out their textbooks and notebooks as they always did to start history. Gregory turned to observation mode. Dr. Bankster got up from behind his desk as he did to start every class.

"Please pull out your homework. I will come by and pick it up from you," Dr. Bankster said as he walked to the first row of desks in the room.

A pit formed in Gregory's stomach. This was new.

Up until today, the homework procedure had always been to drop off your sheet in a basket by the door when class was done. As other students hurried to find their work in their backpacks, Gregory began to sweat. He had nothing to turn in, of course, but that hadn't mattered last week: It was pretty easy to walk out of the room without being noticed. This was harder.

Dr. Bankster moved from student to student, collecting papers. Finally, he arrived at Gregory. He waited. He waited. And he waited. "Your homework, Mr. Korenstein-Jasperton?"

"I don't have any," Gregory finally said.

"You did not do your homework?" Dr. Bankster shook his head. "And would you please tell me and the class why?"

Framed! On the spot! This was not how the day was supposed to go at all. Often, this would be the

121

moment when Gregory would take the path of least resistance and change the subject or go with the flow. It was so tempting to make up an excuse. But this new policy by Dr. Bankster made him angry. It was, again, a teacher using power, in this case to embarrass students. They could no longer hide but had to publicly show their homework prowess. Or at least that's how it seemed to Gregory at that moment in time, and it was enough to tip him over the edge of indecision.

"I'm on strike." Gregory said it firmly . . . but not too loudly. Dr. Bankster didn't move. After a beat, Gregory spoke quite loudly: "I'm on a homework strike."

The silence that followed was overwhelmingly loud. Finally, Dr. Bankster moved on to collect more homework, leaving the statement to hang in the air for just long enough that Gregory thought he'd explode.

"Can you tell us, Gregory, why you are on strike?" Dr. Bankster said, continuing to gather the other students' papers.

All eyes were on him, Gregory knew. He could see Alex giving him a big thumbs-up of encouragement. Benny shook his head slowly and sort of chuckled. And

Ana locked eyes with him and gave him a smile. All told, it was enough.

"We have too much homework. No one gives us a choice about it. It isn't fair. We, too, have rights, Dr. Bankster, and I'm on strike to make things change." Gregory hoped the Yertle reference would be helpful in some way, even if it was just to sidetrack his teacher a little to a Seuss conversation.

"Yes. Well. Is there anyone else who would like to receive a zero on their homework along with Gregory?" Dr. Bankster said, holding up the collected homework. "I'll gladly return your papers to you right now."

There were no takers.

"Good luck with your efforts," Dr. Bankster said to Gregory directly before starting in on the day's lesson.

Gregory shrank in his seat, hoping he'd disappear. He didn't.

Still visible as he joined his classmates on the walk downstairs, Gregory tried to move to the comfort of his friends. He felt like an idiot. What had he been thinking? He was now a laughingstock, called out by Dr. Bankster on his foolishness.

"You're awesome," Elena Todd, seventh-grade class president, said to Gregory as he moved past her, trying to catch up to Alex.

"Crazy idea, man," Boris Masterson, captain of the basketball team, said, and thumped Gregory's shoulder so hard he almost fell down the steps.

"Let me know how I can help," Chuck Dorris— all-around cool kid for no discernible reason as far as Gregory had ever been able to detect—chimed in as they rounded the landing and headed for the third floor.

"You could stop doing your homework," Gregory replied. "Join me."

Chuck quickly blended back in with the crowd on the stairs. Maybe, Gregory thought, Chuck never even heard the request. Up ahead Gregory saw Alex, Ana, and Benny waiting for him on the third floor. He joined them and watched the rest of the class go past. A few more students gave Gregory a thumbs-up or offered encouragement. Then Brock Osterstund, definer of cool, walked past with a shake of the head.

"Dork," Brock said, and the few kids walking with him laughed.

"Awesome and dork are the same, right?" Gregory said when he and his friends had a brief moment alone.

"I'm proud of you," Ana said. "You're a man of your word, and my dad says that's the most important thing."

"More important than grades?" Gregory asked.

"Big picture, GK. Not day-to-day." Ana grinned.

"I do admire your bravery, Gregory," Benny said. "Can you tell me what's next?"

"Surviving." And Gregory was only half joking.

"Accelerating, dude. Word's gonna spread. Your idea is gonna take flight!" Alex led the friends toward their next class. "Or you'll be like Superman with kryptonite strapped to him and tumble from the sky. But it'll be fun to watch anyway."

"I need your help after school. Thirty minutes off from homework, maybe? Can you do that for me?" Gregory's eyes sparkled. "It's time to accelerate."

There were lots of reasons Gregory was glad to have history first period. Dr. Bankster was usually interesting, so that was helpful, but most of all, it got a tough class out of the way so the whole day felt like going downhill. Today, however, there was a real downside— his strike was public knowledge, and word was spreading fast.

At lunch, Gregory saw people looking at him on a day he hadn't spilled anything or broken a plate with a loud clatter. And by the last class of the day, English, he knew Dr. Bankster had been talking too.

"Gregory K.," Mr. Ahearn, his English teacher, said sadly without even asking him to hand in his homework. "I enjoy your essays. And I don't enjoy giving out zeros. I look forward to the return of your efforts in my class."

"Mr. Ahearn, I am still giving effort in your class," Gregory protested.

"Partial efforts. Partial grades." Mr. Ahearn shrugged.

After school, Gregory split from his friends with the promise to catch up later. They went off to do homework at Ana's. Gregory needed some time alone to get his thoughts in order. And, while it wouldn't be quite as helpful as it had been for years when he went there with Kelly, there was one place where he always felt comfortable: the Slice.

To a typical customer, not much had changed about the Slice since Kelly's mom had sold it. You could still order coffee and get great dessert. You sat at the same tables with the same chairs. There was still a happy buzz about the place that welcomed you in. To Gregory, though, the differences were what stood out: new recipes, new font on the menu, new photos on the walls, no Kelly or her mother.

Still, it was a happy place for him, and a place he was always welcome. In fact, as part of her sales agreement, Kelly's mom had insisted that Gregory K. receive a free chocolate chip cookie every time he came in. He tried not to take advantage of the kindness, but some days . . . well . . . some days you needed a cookie. And this was a some day if there ever was one.

Armed with a cookie and a glass of milk, Gregory sat at the table where he'd done homework with Kelly hundreds of times. She wasn't there, of course, and it made him a bit sad. Then again, he also wasn't doing homework, even though it looked like he was. Instead, he was working on two documents—a list of questions people were already asking him and, more importantly, a manifesto. All the good strikes had a manifesto or list of reasons and solutions, Gregory had learned, so any path to success included him creating one too.

With a quick, confident stroke of his pen, Gregory wrote HOMEWORK on the blank white sheet of paper in front of him. Then he paused. For a long time. Eventually, Gregory put the cookie on top of the word, then traced around it with his pencil. He lifted the cookie up and drew an angled line through the circle his tracing had left behind. Once again, he had the no-homework sign, but this time he added to the bottom of it—#HOMEWORKSTRIKE.

It might not be a manifesto, but it was a keeper. He flipped the paper over, grabbed another sheet, and started writing.

Powered by the cookie, Gregory wrote up his thoughts before rejoining his friends at Ana's. In a bit of solidarity, they had hurried through their work in order to give him the thirty minutes he'd asked for.

"That's what friends are for," Benny said. "Plus, there was no English homework today because the Xerox machine was broken."

"So, look, I hate to say it, but Dr. Bankster made me think a lot this weekend and today." Gregory sat at the table with his friends. "I can't do this alone. I'm gonna need other people to go on strike with me."

"Don't look at me, dude. I'm just here for logistical support," Alex said quickly.

"Well, maybe you'll agree with what I stand for." Gregory pulled out the paper he'd been working on and read aloud.

"A Declaration of Independence. Let all ye who hear this . . ."

Ana interrupted him, laughing. "Did you say 'ye'?"

"Not working for you?" All his friends shook their heads no. "Okay, fine. I was going for a whole old-fashioned thing."

"Ye need to suck us in, GK. Ye don't push us away." Alex drummed on his notebook with two pencils. Gregory returned to his reading.

"I will no longer do homework outside of school. I will continue to work hard to learn, but I will not let people tell me what I have to do for hours each day after school. I will campaign to make homework illegal again for all students under the age of sixteen. Unless we take a stand, nothing will get better. It won't. Join me, and make today our independence day!" Gregory looked at his friends. "Whatta ye think?"

"It's simple. I like that," Ana said, reaching for a cookie from a plate in the center of the table. "Do you have something I can sign?"

"Are you joining me?" Gregory asked.

"No!" Ana bit the cookie. "I'm just trying to help think things through for you, that's all."

"I don't. I could start with the bottom of this page. I can sign it like John Hancock," Gregory said. "Then wait for other people to follow."

"Let's pretend for a moment that the whole school joins you, Gregory K.," Benny said. "You would need a bigger paper."

"I'll deal with that then. I am thinking one step at a time. I want to make copies and give them to everyone, see what happens," Gregory said.

"People don't want to fail every class," Benny added. "That's where you lose me. And probably most of ye too."

"They don't have to fail," Ana said quietly. All eyes turned to her. "Seriously. They don't. You don't. No one does, mostly."

Ana grabbed her notebook, flipped to a blank page, and quickly drew a nearly perfect circle on it. "I'm not good with math facts and stuff," she said, "but I see things. Look. This circle is your grade. You can get one hundred percent, right?" Ana drew a small wedge in the circle, like a piece of pie. "That's twenty percent of the circle, okay? That's how much homework counts for in most classes, right?"

"Uh . . . if you say so," Gregory said, embarrassed he didn't know.

"So, the other eighty percent of your grade is still in your control. It's papers and tests and participation and who knows what else. But here's the thing" — Ana quickly broke the eighty-percent wedge into ten almost identical pieces by drawing incredibly straight freehand lines on it.

"Forget grades. Teach me how you do that," Alex said. Ana finished the lines.

"Now, think of those lines as making up one hundred percent of the eighty percent. Let's say you get an eighty average on all the rest of the work besides homework." Ana shaded in eight of the smaller segments.

"You'd get a sixty-four," Alex said, doing the math. "You'd pass."

"With a D," Benny added.

"Still passing!" Gregory felt better than he had since the strike began. "Grounded but passing."

"Not much wiggle room," Alex said, looking at the chart. "Average a seventy-four on tests and papers, and you fail."

"That's twenty-six points of wiggle room. And if I average a hundred on everything else . . ." Gregory trailed off. "Okay, fine. If YOU average a hundred, Alex, you'd still get a B, right?"

"Dude. Seriously?" Alex shook his head. "Support staff, remember?"

"Only one problem, really," Ana said. "Homework counts for one-third of our history grade."

"Which means?" Gregory cut to the chase.

"You'd need an A average on the rest to pass," Ana said, and even Gregory deflated.

"An A on his surprise essays?" Slapping his hand down on the table in frustration, Gregory returned to his manifesto. "You know what? That's why I'm on strike. We can learn all the history we're supposed to learn and we still can't pass a class. That's not okay. That's not fair."

"It is fact, though," Benny said.

"Maybe not when I'm through." Gregory grabbed his paper. "Other than *ye*, do I make changes?"

His three friends shook their heads. When they

broke apart to head home for dinner, Gregory walked by the copy shop first. Normally, when he was doing work for school, he asked his parents to pay for it. This time, though, he thought it smart to dig into his own funds.

It was a good feeling, Gregory had to admit, walking to school with a box full of copies of his strike statement. It was like he was carrying two hundred copies of his own personal license to freedom. Such a good feeling, in fact, that he'd had no trouble waking up early in order to get to school before anyone else.

The walk was perfect, with the sun barely up above the horizon. With no one around, Morris Champlin looked even bigger, somehow . . . and it looked asleep.

Gregory put his backpack down beside the door, pulled out a pile of copies, then sat on the front steps, waiting for people to arrive.

The school door opened behind him, and Gregory turned around. It was Principal Macallan, a big, solid, broad-shouldered man who bore a passing resemblance to a tank.

"Gregory Korenstein-Jasperton. Just the man I wanted to see. Won't you come into my office?" The principal's deep voice cut through the morning air.

"Is that a question?" Gregory asked.

"No." Principal Macallan held the door open wide. With a sigh, Gregory gathered up his stuff. He didn't know exactly what was going on, but he was sure of one thing—he'd made the wrong choice, because even breakfast with O was better than getting called to the principal's office. What good could happen there? None, that's what. But that's where he was going right now.

Life throws curveballs. Changeups too —
They leave me full of doubt.
But whatever life brings
I'll take my swings
And hope I don't strike out.

8

When he was learning to spell, Gregory had been taught all sorts of tricks like "*i* before *e* except after *c* or when sounded like *a* as in *neighbor* or *weigh*" and "change a *y* to *ie* when making a plural." He'd also learned that a *principle* was something you stand for and a *principal* was your "pal." That had made sense to him in elementary school, but here in seventh grade, he was pretty dubious.

As he followed his principal, Gregory noticed that Macallan tilted as he walked, his tree-trunk legs thumping along. Before turning into the school offices, Macallan led Gregory past a big trophy case with all of Morris Champlin's past exploits on display.

"Bear Pride!" Macallan said, patting the glass. "That's your brother's corner over there." Macallan pointed to the back left, where a slew of trophies and plaques showed how big a geek his brother was: City Math and Ready Writing and individual honors at Academic Decathlon and many others Gregory chose to forget.

Eventually, the two arrived at the school offices. While the rest of the school was quiet, the whole crew who really kept things running were already in and working. A few eyed Gregory with sympathy, but most took care of their work and paid him no attention. Macallan led him into the corridors of offices that students referred to as "the maze" until finally getting to his own office. He let Gregory in first, then followed him into the room. Even though the door was open, Gregory shrank in his seat once the principal entered the room, his big presence leading to claustrophobia.

"So, Gregory, how are you this morning?" Macallan squeezed into his oversize desk chair.

"I'm good, Principal Macallan," Gregory said.

There was a beat of silence, so he pressed on. "And how are you?"

"I am concerned, thank you for asking." Macallan leaned forward, and Gregory instinctively leaned back. "Dr. Bankster told me that you are not turning in your homework. He also informed me that you think there is too much homework given out each day."

The principal paused, and Gregory wasn't sure if it was time to respond or not. There had been no question asked, true, but there was an opportunity to mention his issues and maybe, just maybe, find an ally in Principal Macallan. Maybe he was unaware of how much work was going home with his students? Maybe he had been trying to stem the tide, but no one else had ever complained so he couldn't make progress. Maybe . . .

"I just want you to know, Gregory, that your teachers are all among the best at what they do. I trust that if they give you work, there is a reason. And I want you to know that I back them one hundred and ten percent." The principal's beefy hand came down on his metal desk, and the hollow boom bounced from wall to wall and through Gregory's head.

Gregory wanted to point out that Ms. Packard, the

math teacher, would say that 110 percent was silly, and that Mr. Ahearn would say that the *all* before *among* was truly unnecessary. But his calf hurt when those thoughts came to his mind, so he said the only safe reply he could think of: "I'm not mad at the teachers."

"You are disrespecting them when you don't do the work they ask for," Macallan said.

"That's not what I'm trying to do," Gregory said. He wondered if he should mention that he wasn't simply not doing homework but that he was intentionally going on strike. Dr. Bankster, it seemed, hadn't told the principal everything.

There was probably a reason for Bankster's choice, and if he could figure out what it was, that would be helpful. So why wouldn't Bankster say anything? Most likely because he didn't take the strike seriously. Because he saw the only problem as a pesky kid not doing homework. Once again, Gregory thought, teachers were defining him rather than letting him define himself. Gregory went from anxious about Macallan to mad at the whole situation. And determined. While lost in thought, Gregory missed a bit of what his principal was saying to him and only tuned in when Macallan thumped his palm against the desktop again.

"Regardless, it is what you are doing," Macallan was saying. "So consider me your pal, Gregory K., when I suggest to you that disrespect and incomplete work is not a path to success at Morris Champlin or anywhere in life. Show Bear Pride, and make us Bears proud."

Again, Gregory was unsure what to say or whether to say anything. But he knew what he wanted to do. He wanted to get back in front of the school and give out his flyers. He wanted to rile up the Bears, and he figured the best path was to say nothing but "I'll try, sir."

Macallan seemed satisfied, at least if the double hand slap on the table meant anything. A few seconds later, he'd sent Gregory on his way.

In hindsight, Gregory knew that leaving the principal's office and handing out flyers about his strike was not necessarily the best choice he could've made. But at the moment, he was fired up. No one cared about the kids, it was clear, and it was time to stand up and change that.

Gregory strode back through the maze, only getting lost twice, then headed to the front of the school. He handed out flyers until history time. He'd missed a few people early on when he was in the principal's office, but when Elena Todd took a flyer and didn't throw it immediately on the ground, Gregory knew the word would be spread far and wide.

And hopefully, that was a good thing, that showed he was acting with Bear Pride. Or at least a good thing.

Without question, Gregory and his strike were the buzz of the lunchroom. "Of course," Benny noted, "there is no sporting event this week."

Still, it was a rare day when jocks and band members and class officers walked by and gave Gregory a high five when they passed. Actually, it was a never-before day.

"You're totally right," Elena Todd said as she stopped by Gregory's table. "We should have a say in how we use our time."

Not that Elena or anyone stayed longer than that, but still. Lunch was pretty fun, and the whole day felt like progress. A few teachers gave him the stinky eyeball, sure, but for the most part there was lots of what appeared to be support.

"Dude, you gotta get people to sign up and join

you," Alex said as they were leaving school for the day. "You're on fire!"

So Gregory headed to the bottom of the steps, pulled out a notebook and pen, and as his fellow students came by, he said, "Join me on strike!"

Suddenly, Gregory understood what it must be like to be a magnet repelling another magnet. People took off like a shot when he offered them the pen. Soon people were giving him a wide berth, though occasionally yelling out encouragement or . . .

"Good luck, Gregory K.," Chuck Dorris said as he passed without slowing down. "If you can get me an extra three hours a day to play video games, you'll be my hero."

"Not exactly the point, Chuck," Gregory said to the air where Chuck had been.

As the flow of students dwindled, Alex came over to Gregory and made a big show of walking into a "wall" a couple feet from him. "Whoa!" Alex repeatedly pretended he was being stopped by an invisible barrier as he tried but failed to reach his friend. "Dude, you shoulda taken down the force field first."

"Now you tell me?" Gregory tried to sound cheery, but he was seriously bummed.

"Maybe folks need to think about it for a while." Alex broke through the invisible wall and stood next to his friend.

"You've been thinking about it. I don't see your signature here." Gregory pointed to the notebook.

"GK, you don't see anyone's signature there!" Alex laughed. Gregory did not.

"Yeah, but they're not my friends," Gregory muttered then took a deep, long breath. "I bet everyone forgets by the end of tomorrow."

"I doubt that," Alex said. Gregory shrugged, less sure. "Now, I gotta go, dude. Go do some homework or something."

"Ha-ha," Gregory said, shoving his notebook back in his backpack. There'd be no homework for him today, of course. Instead, he was going home to read the books Dr. Bankster had given him earlier. So much about the strike was making sense to him, but the lack of people joining in was clearly a problem. Maybe there was something he was missing. Because if not, the strike was never going to make an impact beyond his report card.

For Gregory, Wednesdays were usually only notable because his mother explored new recipes. As a day, it was generally no better or worse than other days, and in general, it was just a plain old day.

This particular Wednesday dawned the same as usual. Breakfast was uneventful, and the walk to school was too, except for the fact that Alex only communicated by whistling. But even that wasn't totally unusual.

At school, Gregory's fears of no real traction were proven true. He and Alex hung out in front of the school before classes started, and no one came up asking for more information or saying they would join him. It was disappointing, though Gregory was pleased that at least a few kids looked his way.

In history class, Dr. Bankster circled around again for homework, taking an odd path to finish up with Gregory.

"Everyone else has turned in their work, Mr. Korenstein-Jasperton," Dr. Bankster said as he held out his hand, waiting for homework he knew would not be coming. "Apparently, no one else finds homework as big a problem as you do. That is good to know, don't you think?"

For some reason, the comment really crushed Gregory's spirit, and even though Dr. Bankster's lesson was as entertaining as always, Gregory didn't participate in class. Instead, he began thinking about ways to end the strike without looking like a fool or without having to do too much extra work to regain his grades. He was lost in those thoughts as the class bell rang, and if it hadn't been for the shrill sound, he probably wouldn't have heard his teacher's last words of the morning.

"In addition to your already assigned homework, you will all write an essay on how much or how little you value doing homework. Share at least two quotes from figures in American history about the value of homework, as well. Make sure you have a topic sentence, a minimum of three paragraphs, and two hundred words, and, as always, write in complete sentences with excellent grammar." Dr. Bankster seemed to gain fuel based on the dismayed reactions. "These are due Friday."

Well, Gregory thought, he might end his strike . . . but not this week!

Dr. Bankster kept speaking to the class, though he looked straight at Gregory. "This paper is, as is all work in this class, a part of your grade. Keep that in mind, please."

As the students finished filing out of the classroom, only Gregory and Dr. Bankster were smiling, and, it seemed to Gregory, for very different reasons.

"People are saying the essay is your fault," Benny said as he joined Gregory at lunch a little later. "I can understand the argument, though I believe Dr. Banskter is solely responsible for his own actions."

"Nooo. I directly influence him, just like I always have," Gregory said, annoyed. "People really blame me?"

"Why else would a teacher be speaking of homework right now? That's the logic, anyway." Benny carefully opened his lunch bag and placed his sandwich, cookie, and apple in a neat line.

Ana brought her food over to join the two boys. "Can I sit here?" she asked with a smile. "Or will you make me write an essay about why this is a good seat choice?"

"I will. And you need to find five sources that agree with you," Gregory said, clearing off room for Ana and her tray.

"There isn't even one, Gregory K.," Ana said.

"Why did I ever think this strike was a good idea?" Gregory wondered. He absentmindedly chewed on his lunch. "All it's proving is that not only don't adults care what kids think, but kids don't care either."

"Maybe you need to practice patience," Ana said. "Every day you don't do homework with us, I'm a day closer to joining you."

"When I finished history at midnight on Sunday, I had a similar thought," Benny added. "Though I urge you not to mention that to my mother."

"So, what would it take?" Gregory picked at his food. "If I can't even convince my friends . . ."

"Start with your enemies," Ana said.

"I don't even have those!" Gregory shrugged. "Now, if I used my mind control powers to have Dr. B. give out more homework every day, that could do it."

"Yo, dude," Alex said as he approached through the lunchroom carrying a huge pile of papers. "You're famous!"

With a thump, Alex dropped the papers on the friends' table. It was then that Gregory realized that they weren't just papers, but they were papers. As in the school paper. As in . . .

"No. Way." Gregory grabbed the top copy and stared at it, mouth agape. There he was on the bottom of the front page, standing in front of the school trying to get people to sign his notebook. Above him was the headline "Morris Champlin Seventh Grader Goes on Homework Strike."

"I took that pic yesterday. Hope you don't mind." Alex sat down beside Gregory. "You're news, dude."

Eyes scanning the page, Gregory read the article. It continued inside the paper, so he flipped the page and kept on reading. His friends watched his face, noting each raised eyebrow, each tightened nostril. Finally, Gregory put the paper down and . . .

"Awesome!" The smile on Gregory's face could've powered the heat lamps in the cafeteria. "You got every point just right, Alex."

"You never stop talking about it, GK. It wasn't hard." Alex grinned.

"Here's my favorite part," Gregory said, flipping the paper over at the fold, revealing fancy versions of the circular charts that Ana had drawn him before. " 'I think everyone just assumed I'd fail all my classes. Now they see I don't have to. They don't have to.'"

Gregory turned to Ana. "Did you do these?"

Ana nodded. "I forgot how much I missed doing graphics and stuff. I made the time."

"I liked the Dr. Bankster part best, I think," Alex said.

"It was great!" agreed Gregory before reading aloud: "'A single voice talking is how most history starts, said Dr. Roger Bankster, before refusing to confirm whether or not Gregory Korenstein-Jasperton had turned in homework for seven successive days.'"

"It would seem to me," Benny said, still eating away, "that word will be spreading now, Gregory K. It would be time to capitalize."

"Teachers get the paper this afternoon, and we put the rest out before school tomorrow," Alex said. "Be prepared."

"Awesome" was all Gregory could say. He stared at the paper again—his picture and story on the front page. It looked great. "Totally awesome."

Gregory was sure he didn't touch the ground on his walk home. He left his friends at Benny's house to do their homework, though Gregory did stop in to have some dumplings and review his science notes for an upcoming test. Still, he wanted to hurry home and get ready for tomorrow when, he and his friends had all agreed, he needed to stand outside before school again.

By the time he got home, Gregory's brain was full of scenarios—students lining up behind him, teachers stopping homework, Principal Macallan agreeing he'd made the Bears proud.

He walked in the door and headed to his room, passing the open dining room door on his way.

"Hey," O said from the dining room table. "Great picture."

Gregory walked on by for a few steps but then couldn't help himself. He stopped, turned toward the door, and shouted back, "What picture?"

From inside the dining room, O thrust out a copy of the *Morris Champlin News* with Gregory on the front page. "This picture."

"How'd you get that?" Gregory asked. He began shifting nervously from leg to leg, though he wasn't totally sure why.

"I love to read about my little brother," O said. "And I know Mom and Dad will love this article too."

"What?" Gregory asked, turning white.

"I'm sure they support your strike, don't they?" O asked with a deadpan expression firmly affixed.

"They don't know about it yet. I was going to tell them," Gregory mumbled.

"No worries. I took care of that for you," O said, walking past Gregory in the hall.

Nothing, Gregory thought, *ever goes according to plan anymore.* He dropped his backpack on the ground, pulled out a notebook and a pen, and wrote: Dear Mom and Dad—I am running away to the moon. I love you, Gregory.

About to rip the paper out, Gregory instead flipped the notebook shut. The moon was impractical. Instead, he grabbed all his stuff, hurried to his room, closed the door, and curled up under his blanket. It was safe there . . . at least for the time being.

I said, I'm allergic to homework.
It makes me cough and wheeze.
You send me home
with mounds to do,
And I just snuff and sneeze.

My teachers would never believe me.
"Allergic? We think not.
Maybe see a doc," they'd laugh,
"And you can get a shot."

Today my teachers aren't laughing,
And I don't mean to gloat,
But they can't give me homework now:
I've got a doctor's note!

The patterns on the underside of Gregory's blanket were quite intricate, and he studied them until he could have traced them with his eyes closed. But it was almost dinner, and he knew his hiding time was about done.

Gregory hadn't spent all his time in his room in bed. He'd tried calling Kelly, but she was off at dance class. He'd read more on the newsboys' strike in a chapter that Dr. Bankster hadn't marked for him. He'd even done a fast draft of an essay about the value of homework to him, trying to clarify his thoughts. But eventually, he'd gone into hiding, awaiting the inevitable.

A knock at his door caused him to pop his head out from under the covers.

"Nobody's home," Gregory said to the door.

"Then I'll just let myself in," his mother said from the other side. And after a moment or two, that's just what she did.

"I'm sorry, Mom." Gregory sat up in his bed, still clutching the blanket around himself. His mom came over and sat on the foot of it. "I should have told you what I was doing."

"Yes" was all his mom said.

"I thought you wouldn't let me do it," Gregory said. His mother's breathing filled the quiet.

"So, you just didn't say anything? Not much of a long-term strategy, was it?" His mom's gentle tone led Gregory to emerge from his cocoon a little more.

"No," Gregory said. "But this strike, Mom? It is about the long term."

"Believe it or not, I get that," his mom said. "Though your father and I are bit worried about the short term too."

"I'm not going to fail out of school, if that's what you mean. Did O show you the graphs?" Gregory knew the answer as soon as he'd asked.

"No, of course not." His mother laughed. "But we've looked at them since then. Still . . ."

"I'm working really hard in every class. I'm participating, doing the tests and all the work at school. If I keep that up, I'll pass every class. And I'm learning the material, Mom. I'm not being rude. I'm not being disrespectful. I'm practicing civil disobedience, that's all." Gregory pointed at the homework list on his board. "And that's why."

"I know you're working hard. If you weren't, I wouldn't be smiling. But there are consequences for your actions, so I'm not sure that's the point," his mom said.

"Right. Because the point is always that kids don't have rights, and you're going to tell me you know what's best for me, I bet. And I shouldn't be upsetting teachers and skipping homework, and you're maybe even right." Gregory leaned forward, an intensity in his tone that he hoped made his mother listen even more closely. "But three hours of homework a day, Mom? Three hours of work I don't always understand why or how or what for? Short term it was bad, and long term it was badder."

"I know you see it that way . . ." His mom picked her words carefully. "It's just that . . ."

"Go ahead and ground me, then. Take away my phone. Make O my tutor. I'm not stopping." Gregory surprised himself with the statement, and his mom surprised him with her laughter.

"Oh, Gregory. I think the strike is totally awesome." His mom reached over and mussed up her son's hair. "I'm not going to ask you to stop."

"You're not?" Gregory's eyes went wide as Frisbees.

"No. And I'll work on your father so he won't either. Not yet, anyway." His mother breathed deeply. "I just want to make sure you know the stakes. It's not an easy thing you're doing, you know."

"Yeah. I'm figuring that out."

"I didn't try it until college, so I'm impressed," his mother said as she stood up.

"Wait. What did you do in college?" Gregory asked.

"Oh, the specifics aren't important. They were good causes. And, you know, I was young and believed." His mother shrugged. "It was a long time ago."

"How'd it go?" Gregory studied his mother's face, looking for any hint.

"I learned a lot."

"Like what?" Gregory pressed on.

"Sometimes you have to make a big mess, and sometimes you can't even clean it up. But when it's a good cause, that's not a high price to pay. Long term, anyway." His mom walked toward the door. "Now I have to finish cooking. If I leave that quinoa-alfalfa non-meatloaf in the oven too long, it won't taste good with the green gravy."

Gregory suspected he shouldn't trust his emotions right now since Weird Wednesday dinner sounded delicious, but he felt great, particularly surprising since he still felt terrible about not having told his parents to begin with. He'd rectify that now, telling his parents everything, even if it meant hearing O make fun of him throughout dinner. It probably wouldn't be fun, though now that he thought about it, it would most likely distract him from the green gravy, and that, for certain, was a good thing.

Dinner was better than Gregory expected it to be. Not the food, of course, but the fact that no one, not even O, told him his idea was terrible. Sure, O pointed out that federal law limits the rights of students, so unlike with a typical strike, there was no legal protection available to Gregory, but that wasn't even an issue at the moment.

His mom and dad listened and asked good questions. His mom offered lots of enthusiastic ideas, though he declined her suggestion that he needed a theme song. Kay was remarkably quiet until the very end of dinner.

"You're like my own Gandhi or Thoreau," she said, looking at Gregory with a respect she usually only showed when speaking of his poetry. "And you need cool slogans and signs."

"You do," his mother added. "You can't get a crowd chanting 'we have too much homework and we'd really like a little less, please, thanks.' You need short and sweet."

While Gregory didn't fully understand the first part of what Kay had said, he knew his sister and mother were right about the latter. He had some ideas about what he wanted a sign to say, but his artistic talent was low enough that he didn't think he should try on his own. Still, he was pretty sure he knew who could help—Ana. So after dinner and a quick phone call to make sure it was okay, he headed over to Ana's apartment with a few pieces of poster board Kay had left over from her last science fair project.

"I need a sign for the morning," Gregory said, handing Ana a sheet of paper with his sketch on it. "And I want it to look like I didn't make it, because if I make it, it'll look lousy."

Ana led Gregory through her apartment to the garage door. She opened it and walked inside, but Gregory stopped in the doorway. The garage was full of canvases on easels with a few works in progress among the empty ones. The walls were packed with art—paintings and sketches, framed and unframed. The splashes of paint on the drop cloths on the floor looked like Jackson Pollock had visited, and the vibrant colors of the works on the wall screamed in contrast to the darker hues of the works in progress.

"This is incredible," Gregory said, stepping inside. "Is this your dad's stuff? Your mom's?"

"Nope. Just mine," Ana said as she grabbed one of the pieces of poster board from Gregory. He wouldn't let go, but only because he was so busy staring around the room.

Gregory's eyes jumped around, taking in the colors and shapes and the textures of paint on paint. Some of the work looked like exercises or practice—pictures of trees, landscapes, pieces of fruit. Some were done in paints, others in pencil, and more in brightly colored markers. They were well done, at least as far as Gregory could tell. But his eyes mostly stayed on the paintings of abstract designs, of buildings that appeared to be optical illusions, of crazy fantasy landscapes.

"You're kidding me, right? All yours?" Gregory finally relinquished his hold on the board as he stopped looking around.

"You write. I paint. No big deal," Ana said as she set the poster board on an easel.

"It's a big deal to me. I love this stuff," Gregory said. "You're so good!"

"Thanks," Ana said softly.

"How often do you paint?" Gregory saw a pile of prepared canvases, all blank. "Like, how long to fill these?"

"Dunno. School messes with my ability to paint all day long." Ana tried to joke, but Gregory immediately recognized the tone, because it was a common tone for him too. He walked over to Ana, unsure of what to say.

After too much silence, Ana grabbed a box of markers. "Let me get this done for you, okay?"

"Not much of a use of your talents. I feel like I'm saying 'Hey, Michelangelo, wanna help me paint my garage?'" Gregory paused. "Although if I make a sign, no one will be able to read it."

"That wouldn't help your case at school, I'm thinking," Ana said. "It's no biggie, GK. At least it got me out here on a school night."

That was so sad, Gregory thought. And, frankly, it was a perfect illustration of why he was doing what he was doing. It wasn't just about him. There was a greater good. As Ana began to work on his sign, he imagined her having hours extra each day to work on her paintings. This, he hoped, would tide him over if things turned bad again. Not that he saw how that would happen at this point, but you just never knew . . .

Early the next morning, Gregory grabbed a granola bar and headed off for school, even though the buzz in the house was that Dad was making his famous pancakes. Gregory carried the three signs Ana had made for him, with two portable easels to use as stands strapped on top of his backpack. One of the signs had been taped to a long piece of tree branch so he could hold it in one hand.

Arriving at the school before any other student, Gregory got to work. He measured out twenty feet from the front doors of the school so that no one could accuse him later on of obstructing the business from operating . . . a law he'd read about while studying strikes . . . then paced off five more feet to be sure, ending up in a patch of grass just beyond the sidewalks leading to Morris Champlin. It was perfect.

Quickly, Gregory set up one easel and placed the biggest of the three signs on it—a sign bearing the word *HOMEWORK* with a big "No" sign through it. Below that—in perfectly readable printing, Gregory marveled—it said *#homeworkstrike.*

As Gregory set up the second easel, he thought he caught sight of eyes looking out at him from a room in the school, but he couldn't spot them when he looked again. He returned to the task at hand and put up the second sign. This one said *I Want My Voice to Be Heard* at the top. The rest of the poster was blank. Gregory reached into his backpack, pulled out a handful of colored markers he'd borrowed from Ana, and laid them on the shelf of the easel. He looked at the array of colors and picked up the red marker, uncapping it.

"Hold on a second, young man," a gruff voice said, causing Gregory to twist around in surprise. He relaxed when he saw Alex, who then continued in his fake voice. "Get off my lawn, you pesky kid!"

"What are you doing here?" Gregory asked.

"We reporters follow the news," Alex said, pulling out his cell phone. "And maybe Ana told me and maybe I wanted to get some pictures, just in case something big happens."

"Yeah, that's the thing that was missing at the signing of the Declaration of Independence — a photograph. All we get is those lousy paintings." Gregory laughed. "Are you serious?"

"Haven't been so serious since I forced you to watch the last season of *Doctor Who*, dude." Alex lined up a shot of Gregory though his camera. "Now, as you were, John Hancock."

Taking a deep breath, Gregory returned to the nearly blank poster, put the marker on it, and signed his name in big red letters. He took a step back to look at it as Alex took a few steps forward to join him.

"If you become famous, you are so signing my original photographs," Alex said, checking the images on his phone.

"Famous? Not so likely." Gregory capped the marker. "Check this out. Look what Ana can do."

Gregory grabbed the tree branch attached to the poster board, lifted it, and rotated it around to Alex. He whistled low, looking at the painting of the figure of Justice holding scales . . . with a school on one side, holding the scale down, and a slew of students standing on the other side, lifted high in the air. Below it were the words *We, too, should have rights!*

"She's amazing," Alex said softly.

"Dude," Gregory said, "you like her! I mean, I think you *like* like her."

"What? I'm just talking about her drawings here, GK," Alex said, his face turning a shade to match the red marker Gregory had signed with.

"No worries." Gregory threw his hands up in the air as if he was backing off. "But she is pretty cool."

"I'm gonna go hand out the paper. You need to focus." Alex walked off, face still beet red.

For a few minutes, Gregory was alone again in front

of the school. It looked massive to him from here, and suddenly Ana's picture didn't seem so off the mark. A group of students was no match for a giant institution and all the power it represented. Of course, that's how it had seemed to the newsboys and the steelworkers and so many others too.

Slowly, students began to appear, dropped off by parents or walking in from nearby. A few kids eyed Gregory nervously as he held Ana's sign aloft and paced back and forth in front of his two posters. Even more gave him a very wide berth.

A few minutes later, Alex and the rest of the newspaper staff came out on the front steps of the school, handing out the *Morris Champlin News*. As always happened when the paper came out, kids glanced at the front cover and a lot of them dropped the paper straight in the trash. This time, though, more kids than normal were reading . . . and looking at Gregory . . . then looking back at the paper.

He picked up his pacing pace and started shouting, "Hey, hey. Ho, ho. You say homework. I say no!" Again and again, Gregory chanted until a small crowd had circled around.

The other voices started in slowly, but the sound started growing. First it was five kids, then twenty, and then it must have been fifty kids or more chanting.

"Hey, hey. Ho, ho. You say homework. I say no!"

Alex ran around taking pictures. Bodies pressed in around Gregory as discarded newspapers littered the ground nearby. The energy of the crowd was infectious, and Gregory chanted louder, trying to get the whole student body to join in.

A distorted voice rang out, powered by an electric bullhorn. It was Principal Macallan, and even with the feedback and crackling, his displeasure was clear. "Students. Students, please report to your first-period classes right now."

The chanting dimmed, but it was still audible. Until, "You have three minutes until the school bell rings. If you are not in class, you will be in detention for the next five days."

It was as if the entire school belonged to the track team. Students left Gregory as fast as they had arrived, leaving him alone holding his sign aloft. The two easels had been knocked over, and his stuff was scattered around when he finally realized that Principal Macallan was still standing there, watching all the kids but mostly him.

"Come on, GK." Ana seemed to materialize out of nowhere. "Let's get to class."

"I've got the stands," Benny said, and Gregory wondered where he'd come from.

The three worked quickly, gathering Gregory's stuff and running for the school. They dashed inside, then headed up the stairs to Dr. Bankster's class, puffing as they ran. They rounded the third-floor landing, and Benny stumbled, dropping the easels.

"Go!" Gregory said as he scrambled to pick them up. He knew his friends were helping him out, but if there was detention to be had, it was for him.

He picked up the stands and, with his backpack dangling precariously off his shoulder, he hurried up the last flight of stairs, one of the posters in his hand nearly tripping him. He slid inside Dr. Bankster's room a half second before the bell rang and lay on the floor, panting.

"Good morning, class," Dr. Bankster said without acknowledging the excitement. "Please turn in your homework. And Mr. Korenstein-Jasperton, please take your seat."

It took a few moments for Gregory to collect himself and his stuff. He decided to take two trips, dumping the stands and his backpack at his desk, then coming back to pick up the poster. It was lying facedown on the floor when he got to it, and he peeled it up—it was the *I Want My Voice to Be Heard* poster . . . and there was not a single signature on it.

"Well, well," Dr. Bankster said, standing above Gregory and looking at the blank space on the poster. "You must be very proud."

Gregory was feeling many things, but proud was not one of them.

"Yet I am sure Principal Macallan will not find the little scene today a reason to be Bear proud. And I am sure he'll hold you fully responsible," Dr. Bankster added. "I just thought you'd like to know."

Gregory put the poster against the wall next to his seat and collapsed in a heap. This strike thing was hard work. And what did he have to show for it? At the moment, absolutely nothing.

I left it at home.

It made me weep.

I did other work.

I fell asleep.

I must've lost it.

I did it last week!

What? There was homework?

To me it was Greek.

My printer was dead.

I don't always understand what it's supposed

to teach me or how it helps me and it builds

stress and anxiety and some of it is pretty

boring and we really have way too much of it

so I don't have a life and I don't do it

because I hate it.

It's not due tomorrow?

Yes, my dog ate it.

It took a few minutes, but Gregory finally caught his breath and tried to get into the flow of the class. Dr. Bankster was lecturing about the colonists again, and even though it was interesting, Gregory's eyes kept stealing over to the poster—battered, bruised, and empty.

As Gregory looked around the classroom, he saw a lot of other eyes stealing over to look at the poster too. Most specifically, he saw Ana staring at it.

As Dr. Bankster finished telling a story about the Sons of Liberty, Ana raised her hand.

"Yes, Ana? I'm so glad to see you have a question." Dr. Bankster always loved conversation.

"Why would Principal Macallan be upset that Gregory's asking people to sign a poster saying they want their voices heard?" Ana asked. "Don't we all want our voices heard?"

"And what, may I ask, does this have to do with the Sons of Liberty?" Dr. Bankster sounded unamused.

"Nothing," Ana admitted. "And neither did your homework essay about homework. Uhhhh . . . Dr. Bankster. Sir."

The classroom sounded like someone had switched on a vacuum cleaner as twenty-five kids drew in their breath in surprise all at once. Dr. Bankster, however, simply chuckled.

"Fair enough," the teacher said. "Let me respond with a question right back to you and the whole class. If you all want your voices heard, why didn't you all sign Gregory's poster?"

Elena Todd was the first to raise her hand. "I didn't want to get in trouble."

"Good. Good. Yet why do you think you would've gotten in trouble for saying that you want your voice heard?" Dr. Bankster replied.

"It was a mob scene out there" was Elena's only reply, and Gregory K. could tell by her facial expression that she knew it wasn't a particularly good answer.

Boris Masterson's hand went up like a shot. "My grades matter to me."

"Your work reflects that, Boris." Dr. Bankster paused. "And yet, that was not the question I had asked. You need to make the connections in speech as well as when I request an essay. So again I ask, why did you not say you want your voice to be heard?"

Benny's hand went up next. "It would be easy to think that signing the poster was agreeing with Gregory K. that we should be on strike."

Dr. Bankster nodded agreement. "Guilt by association. Many a colonist was incarcerated for associating with people who were known to be disloyal to the Crown."

"There just seems no point in it," Brock said from his seat at the front. "There's always gonna be homework. And no way a kid like Gregory K. changes that."

"Disbelief in the message or the ability of the message to be heard," Dr. Bankster rephrased. "It is easy for us to expect the status quo to remain the status quo. Efforts to fight it are often wasted efforts. Very true. But let me ask you all by a show of hands . . . how many of you agree with Elena, at least in part. You don't want to get in trouble."

The show of hands was pretty much unanimous.

"But that's a different thing, isn't it?" Ana asked. "There was nothing wrong with standing out there jumping up and down and yelling."

"It has nothing to do with right or wrong. If I don't get in trouble, it makes it safe to agree with me. And if it's safe to agree with me, who knows what happens?" Gregory shook his head. "Intimidation. Isn't that the term, Dr. Bankster, like when the leaders of the steel strike were beaten up so everyone else would feel physically unsafe?"

"Perhaps. Of course, perhaps Principal Macallan's plan is to let this whole thing pass by, since making an example of you runs the risk of bringing attention to you." Dr. Bankster smiled just a little before continuing. "And goodness knows, nobody wants that, Gregory K."

"Right. He wouldn't want me to turn into a Kid Blink type, like with the newsboys strike, and have everyone rooting for me," Gregory said.

"Precisely," Dr. Bankster said.

"That's all just ridiculous," Ana said, getting out of her seat and crossing to the poster. As the rest of the class watched, Ana grabbed a marker and signed the poster too. "Bottom line. I want my voice to be heard."

Ana capped up the marker, then walked over to Benny. He hesitated a long time, but Ana's eyes stayed on him. Finally, he grabbed the marker and went to sign the poster. "Even my parents can't disagree with this, and actually, I don't care if they do." He signed with a flourish, then looked at the poster. After a long moment, he looked over to Gregory. "But for the record, if they do blame me for anything, you get no more dumplings."

"Seems fair," Gregory said, his eyes smiling at the support. Benny handed Gregory the marker. He held it up. "Anyone else think your voice should be heard too?"

By the time the class period was done, Gregory had twenty signatures beneath his, including Ana's, Benny's, and Elena's. He didn't know exactly what that meant overall, but at least he was no longer alone.

Except, as Gregory quickly learned, when he and his classmates were walking down the hall together and Principal Macallan was walking the other way, he would once again regain his repelling-magnet force and find himself unfriended. Alone, he realized, was something he'd be quite a lot until this was all over.

Even Principal Macallan showed no interest in Gregory at the moment, instead focusing on a clipboard full of papers he was carrying. He nodded and said hello to people as he passed, but he didn't give Gregory a second look. His classmates, however, didn't rush back to join him.

At lunch, Gregory sat with Ana, Benny, and Alex at their usual table off to the side of the typical buzz.

"Twenty-nine seventh graders have signed my poster!" Gregory said, taking his seat and giving Alex a shoulder punch. "Wanna make it thirty, dude?"

"GK, man, don't take this the wrong way. I'm not signing. I'm treating this like a news story, and reporters shouldn't be part of the news," Alex said.

"Or, you know, maybe you just do everything you want anyway and homework's not a big deal," Gregory said. "It's okay. Do what you want."

"I want to make sure your voice is heard saying you want your voice heard, you know?" Alex replied.

"I heard that, man." Gregory dug in to his lunch. As he was about to take a bite, a short-haired, small, quiet-looking eighth grader Gregory had never spoken to before came up to the table.

"I heard about your poster at recess. Can I sign it?" the eighth grader said.

"Absolutely," Gregory replied. He grabbed the poster from where he'd leaned it behind his chair and swung it up onto the table. Ana pulled out a few markers.

"Pick your favorite color," she said.

"You'll be the first eighth grader to sign, my friend," Gregory said, then when he saw the flash of fear in the boy's eyes, he realized it wasn't necessarily his best lead-in. "But you won't be the last," he added encouragingly.

The student picked green and signed his name. "I want my voice to be heard," he said as he walked away.

All lunchtime long, a slow, steady trickle of kids came by the table, where normally no one ventured. Each one signed the poster. Some were silent. Others offered encouragement. And others . . .

"Might as well sign," Otto Martins, a big, loud eighth grader, said as he came over to the table. "I haven't done homework in years anyway."

"That's not exactly a strike, Otto," Alex said. "That's just not doing homework."

"No diff, man!" Otto said. "Now there's safety in numbers."

By the end of lunch, there were fifty-two signatures on the poster, and white space on it was getting scarce.

"Told you it should've been a scroll," Ana said.

"Perhaps you can attach another board at the bottom?" Benny traced his signature on the board nervously.

"On the side," Gregory said. His friends looked at him quizzically. "Easier to display if we go beyond two or three. It'll look like all those sports banners in the gym this way."

"Bear Pride, dude," Alex said, giving out high fives. "Bear Pride."

It was a celebratory walk to Benny's after school, with the whole homework crew in a great mood. Gregory carried his poster, now eighty-two signatures strong, and every now and then thrust it up into the sky victoriously. Ana carried the #homeworkstrike and Justice posters carefully, but not visibly, while Benny had the extra stands. Alex stopped often to take pictures.

"You did it, GK," Ana said. "You started something."

"Lotta people want their voices heard," Gregory said. "Lotta people."

"Yes. Yes," Benny agreed. "I'm just a little unsure of something."

"What's that?" Gregory spun around and walked backward to listen.

"How, exactly, do we go from here to actually having our voices heard?" Benny hurried on, "No disrespect meant."

"As more kids sign up, people will have to listen," Gregory said. "We get big enough, we can talk to Congress, I figure. But for now, we need to get big enough that they listen to us at school."

"Yes, and what does that look like?" Benny asked. "I'm simply trying to understand."

"Well, we keep talking until they acknowledge the problem. We ask for a way to talk to more people," Gregory said, spinning back to walking forward. "We keep going until something happens."

"The town hall meeting would be perfect," Alex said. "Parents come. Teachers are there."

"It's always on a weekday night and they talk about dull educational issues," Benny said. "And no students have ever spoken."

"So we say we want to speak. Right now they probably won't let us, so we make it so that they have to let us," Gregory said.

"Yes, but even then, why will anyone listen to us?" Benny asked. He stopped walking. "I really do want my voice to be heard. I really do, and I'm willing to take risks to make it so. I just want to understand."

"The truth has a way of being heard, particularly when a group stays united. It really does," Gregory said as he circled back to Benny. "Now, what's on tap today other than making my sign-up poster bigger?"

"Some of us have homework," Benny said, walking again.

"All of us do," Gregory corrected his friend. "But one of us is on strike."

"Science test tomorrow," Ana said. "Math test Monday."

"You know what I haven't figured out?" Gregory asked as the quartet rounded the corner.

"How to leap tall buildings in a single bound?" Alex asked.

"Something that rhymes with George Washington?" Ana added.

"Yes. And yes. And whether or not test review packets count as homework," Gregory said.

"You do them at home, so I'd suggest yes." Benny led the way up the driveway to his house.

"But we don't turn them in for a grade," Ana added.

"Hold on. Are you saying if GK did all his homework but didn't turn it in, that would be okay?" Alex asked.

"Stupid, kinda, but it would still be like a strike, right?" Ana turned to Gregory, hoping for an explanation.

"It's about choice, I think. When it's my choice, it's different," Gregory said. "Look, I'm making this up as I go, but I just know that if I don't look over the review packet, I maybe don't pass the math test. And I really need to pass the math test."

"I think those were your first words as a baby," Alex said, following Benny inside. "But I'll study with you anyway. Homework's light today."

"Except for Dr. Bankster's essay," Benny added. "That you, Gregory Korenstein-Jasperton, are entirely responsible for."

"Ugh, I'm never gonna get that done," Ana said. "I've just accepted that."

"Go on strike," Gregory said totally seriously. "When you're treated unfairly, you have to take action."

"No. You do. I just have to figure out how to keep my grades up," Ana said.

The four friends arrived at Benny's dining room table and threw aside their backpacks and supplies. They all immediately scanned the table, but . . .

"No dumplings!" Alex practically whimpered.

"Let me see what I can find out," Benny said. He took a deep, calming breath and went out of the dining room.

Very carefully, Gregory placed the poster of signatures on the dining room table. It looked gorgeous, he thought, maybe even better than the painted images that Ana made on the Justice poster. Perspective was everything.

"How many sheets do you think you'll fill?" Ana asked, getting her books out of her backpack.

"Depends if everyone signs with such big letters or not. There are eighty-two signatures here, not that I've counted them or anything." Gregory grinned.

"Not in the last two minutes, anyway," Alex laughed.

"If we make the 'I Want My Voice to Be Heard' part a bit smaller and people don't copy my big letters, we could get hundreds on a sheet. And there's maybe four hundred fifty kids in the school, right?" His friends concurred. "So, maybe we fill up one more. Four maximum, but that would mean everyone signs. I'll attach 'em one at a time, and hope for the best."

"And I'll take pictures," Alex said.

Suddenly, Benny's voice could be heard from the other room, sounding far more high-pitched than normal. "But, Mommmm . . ."

"That doesn't sound good," Ana said, concerned.

"It's the sound of Dumplings Crisis, Day One," Alex said.

"Don't make fun, Alex. Imagine if Kelly's mom had

cut off our supply of cookies and pie." Gregory shuddered. "That would've been a disaster!"

The trio of friends spread their notebooks out in front of them, readying for work. Less than a minute later, Benny came in, his face flushed.

"You all have to go now," Benny said.

"What?" Ana replied. "Tests, Benny. We've got tests."

"You have to go," Benny said, head hanging. "I'm sorry."

"But . . . but . . ." Alex went mock-wide-eyed and whimpered again, "Dumplings???!!!!"

Nobody knew exactly what to do, so no one did anything for a moment. Finally, Gregory picked up the poster.

"Someone called your parents, didn't they?" Gregory asked.

"No," Benny said. "It was an email from the school about the morning scene. It was not a phone call."

"The morning? Not even this?" Gregory shook the sign. "Do you know what the email said?"

Benny shook his head sadly. "I only know that it was enough that my mother feels this group is a bad influence on me."

"Homework club is a bad influence?" Ana was incredulous. "You three are the only reason I've made it this far this year!"

"The parental perception is not shared by me in this case. But I have to ask you to leave. Please." Benny was near tears. Gregory was the first to start packing back up. Wordlessly, Ana and Alex followed suit.

It took way too long for them to get organized enough to leave. Anxiety and helplessness hung in the air, slowing everyone down. Finally, Alex led the way out, silently walking past Benny. Gregory searched for words, but came up empty, so he gave a helpless smile as he walked past. Ana followed her friends, but just as she passed Benny she turned back around and gave him a huge hug. She hurried off after Gregory and Alex.

Ana, Gregory, and Alex walked through the afternoon sun in silence. Their pace was glacial, weighed down by math books and thoughts. After a long time, Ana broke the silence.

"That totally sucks," she said.

"It's not your fault, dude," Alex said to Gregory. "You know that, don't you?"

Gregory nodded. "I still feel terrible. And both your parents will get that email, too, whatever it says."

"They'll be proud," Ana said. "Particularly when they find out I wasn't even late for class or anything."

"And I've done nothing to worry about," Alex said quietly.

"I don't really think Benny did either," Gregory said.

The silence returned, and the friends walked slowly to the end of the block. They stopped at the corner and looked from one to another.

"My mom's home today," Gregory said. "We can go work there. No dumplings, though."

"Dumplings," Alex said mournfully. "Poor Benny."

The trio walked through the town, taking their well-trodden shortcuts between yards and on side streets. It was only a ten-minute walk, but today it stretched on longer than normal, at least to Gregory. He was still thrilled about the day but now sad that it had hurt Benny. Plus, he was worried about his own parents' reaction to the email and genuinely curious about what the email said.

He and the gathered crowd at school hadn't done anything illegal, so far as he knew. They hadn't interfered with school at all, and he hadn't heard any reports of teachers being upset or even of anyone being late for class. His best guess was that the email simply made Benny's parents aware of something that wasn't to their liking. Benny always said his parents were super strict, so maybe it was that simple. Whatever it was, though, he hoped his own parents weren't going to be as upset.

When they arrived at his house, Gregory shouted out a quick "hi!" and led the friends straight into the dining room, sorta-kinda-maybe thinking he'd avoid his mom. It didn't work. She arrived a minute or two later, carrying two plates of sliced fruit.

"I wasn't expecting you here today," his mom said, placing the snacks down. "I thought you were at Benny's."

"It didn't work out," Gregory said, feeling none too good about it.

"Sounds like it's been quite a day for you," his mom said.

"What did the email say, Mom?" Gregory asked. "Might as well get it over with."

"Principal Macallan expressed concern that students not get distracted from daily learning. After all, the important state testing period is sometime in the future, and all learning is critical. Something like that," his mother said.

"Really?" Alex said. "That's what he went for?"

"I'm not distracted, Mrs. Korenstein-Jasperton," Ana offered.

"Mom, we're getting together today to study for tests. Distracted?" Gregory's frustration burst out in his tone. "That's so bogus."

"It struck me as a way to sound scary without actually saying anything specific," his mother said. "It's also a warning to you."

"A warning?" Gregory asked, confused.

"Yes. He had some invisible line. You crossed it, and he's telling you to stop pushing." His mother gave a hint of a smile, then switched to a mock whisper. "I thought it was weak."

Gregory laughed with relief. His mother waited a moment, watching the friends. "Now, please, please. Don't let me interrupt studying."

The three friends hurriedly grabbed books as his mother watched. After a bit, Gregory's mother left.

"Distracted from learning?" Gregory whispered. "We didn't do anything!"

"Macallan shot first!" Alex whispered back.

"Can we please start studying," Ana whispered a little too loudly.

The friends turned their attention to their work but a moment later were distracted by the doorbell.

"It's Macallan paying a home visit, I bet," Alex said with a grin.

Even though he kept his eyes on his papers, Gregory could hear the faint sounds of his mother talking with someone at the door. After a bit, the door closed, and two sets of footsteps echoed in the hallway. Gregory looked up as his mother entered the room, followed by a studious-looking twentysomething woman dressed in what Gregory called "grown-up clothes."

"Gregory," his mother said, "This is Liz Magruder. She's a reporter for the *News Leader*."

The *News Leader* was the daily paper for the cluster of small towns where Gregory lived. Everyone read it, even though everyone complained there was never anything in it that they didn't already know.

"Nice to meet you, Gregory," said the reporter. "I understand you're on a homework strike. I'd love to talk to you about it."

Ana, Alex, and Gregory exchanged quick glances.

"I'm the guy who broke the story, ma'am," Alex said, rising up to shake her hand. "Alex Delosa, *Morris Champlin News*."

"I have a copy of your fine work with me," Liz said, shaking Alex's hand firmly.

"Mom?" Gregory said. "What do you think?"

"I think," his mother said softly, "that this is news, and she will do the story whether she talks to you or not."

"Oh," Gregory said, trying to read his mother's tone.

"I am concerned, Gregory, because I am your mother, after all. I don't want you upsetting people or embarrassing anyone, but I also don't want the story to be told by anyone other than you." His mother looked him in the eye. "So, I'll leave the choice up to you."

Liz Magruder stood, pen poised over her note-book, waiting for the go-ahead. Gregory looked at his mother's face, a mix of concern and excitement. He looked around the table at his friends and at the gap where Benny should be sitting.

And he knew what he had to do.

There's a stressful feeling growing here
That no one wants to mention.
If I'm the cause does
that make me
The center of a tension?

11

In the newspaper business, as Alex told Gregory, when you're on the top of the front page, you're "above the fold." That's prime real estate—the most-read stories most days—and that's where Gregory K. and the homework strike ended up in the *News Leader* the next morning. There was even a picture of Gregory with his three signs, before the excitement started, credited to Alex.

When he woke up that morning, however, Gregory didn't know he'd made the paper. Instead, he knew he needed to study his science notes one more time. Losing twenty percent of his grade by being on strike made every other part of the class that much more important, and Gregory was shooting for As when he could get there. He'd studied more for science than he ever had before, in fact, and was poring over his notes when his father came into the dining room, holding the *News Leader*.

His dad tossed the paper over to Gregory but said nothing, instead just sitting down and sipping his coffee. Gregory tried to play it cool, ignoring the paper in favor of his science, but curiosity got the best of him. He looked. He read. He smiled.

"What did you think, Dad?" Gregory asked.

"Your mom says the quotes seem accurate." His father's eyebrows pulled down low on his forehead, tension lines so deep they cast shadows.

Gregory read aloud from the paper, " 'Maybe homework isn't all bad,' Mr. Korenstein-Jasperton said. 'We just have too much of it, and nobody listens when we ask for that to change. Parents say that's just the way it is. Teachers are working so hard, and they get judged on things that they think homework might help us with. And the only laws that protected us have been taken off the books.' Yup. That's accurate all right."

Placing his coffee mug down on the table, Gregory's father rubbed at his temples. "Everything you said makes sense, but I don't really understand why you're saying it."

"Did you do three hours of homework a day when you went to school, Dad?" Gregory put the paper down and looked at his father, studying his face.

"I don't think so. I don't remember. But I certainly had homework." His father took a sip of coffee. "I just don't know what you think will change, Gregory."

"I'm sorry," O said, entering the room carrying a heaping bowl of cereal, "did I just hear 'Gregory' and 'think' in the same sentence?"

"Your brother's famous, O," his father said, pointing to the paper. Gregory gleefully showed his brother the picture and headline.

Many times, Gregory had hated being O's younger brother. He was a tough act to follow in school, for starters. He was not usually very nice at home. But it was also just plain old hard for Gregory ever to do anything that O hadn't already done. Maybe if Gregory was an athlete . . . but he wasn't. He wrote, and he struggled in school, neither of which ever led to much excitement. But this? Well, O had been in the paper before, but never on the front page.

"I like the way your eyes make you look evil,"

O said after a quick glance. Gregory tried to peek at the photo without letting O notice, even though he knew that was exactly what his brother wanted.

"I'm curious what you think about this whole homework . . . thing, O," their father said.

"Homework just is." O shrugged as he placed his bowl down on the table. "And it isn't hard to do it."

"Is that talking for you or talking for everyone?" Gregory asked.

"My name is the Lorax. I speak for the trees and every school-age child in the world," O replied.

"Doesn't matter. I'm not talking about whether it's hard or not. I'm not even talking about whether you learn from it," Gregory said.

"Learn from it? Who said anything about that?" O said through a mouth of cereal.

"So why do it?" Gregory asked. "Why not just stand up and say, 'This is ridiculous and I've got better things to do' and come up with a solution that works for everyone?"

O shook his head sadly. "You still think people listen to kids, don't you? Wait until you're eighteen and can make your own rules. Until then, do what needs to be done and spend your time on things you're good at, like math. Except that's me. For you, I guess . . . well . . . uh . . . eating pie."

"Seems a rather dismal view, actually," Gregory's father said to O. "If you don't speak up, you never get heard no matter what your age. I learned that from your mother, by the way. All I ask, Gregory, is that you treat everyone with respect and that you have a plan."

Gregory smiled at his father, relieved at the reaction. In fact, he realized, he probably owed some of that to O, though it didn't seem time to say "thanks."

After a long pause, Gregory noticed his father was still looking at him. "You do have a plan, don't you?" his dad asked.

"Of course I have a plan!" Gregory blurted out far too quickly.

"Care to share it with me?" his father said.

O grabbed his bowl and headed out of the room. "I'm all ears too. See how interested I . . ." The end of O's sentence disappeared along with the speaker.

Gregory neatened up his science work. "I'll tell you later, if that's okay." Gregory focused on his papers, not his father. "I need to study."

Gregory's dad tapped the newspaper as he stood up.

"You don't look evil, by the way. I think you look kinda handsome."

"Daaaad," Gregory groaned as his father walked by and mussed up his hair.

All told, Gregory knew things had gone well. He quickly packed up his science work and shoved it in his backpack, choosing to leave before things could go worse with his mother. It's not that he expected anything bad, really, but it wasn't time to push his luck.

When Gregory fell into step beside Alex on the hill to school, his friend was grinning ear to ear. "My first credit in the city paper, dude. Sure, it's just a photo, but you know I broke your story."

"I'm just a story to you now, huh?" Gregory laughed. "I remember when I was a friend."

"And I remember when you still did homework. Soon, all those memories will fade away . . ." Alex loped up the hill. "So, what did your dad say?"

"He was okay with it all, really. He just wants to make sure I have a plan." Gregory knelt down to tie his shoe.

"And you told him you did but didn't give him details. And your calf hurt," Alex said, turning around to face Gregory while walking backward up the hill.

"Something like that. Except that I do have a plan. Or a goal, anyway." Gregory finished tying his lace as Alex swung back around as he neared the top of the hill. "If I can just get people to really listen . . ."

Alex stopped dead in his tracks. "Uh, GK? I don't think that's gonna be a problem."

Gregory stood up and headed toward Alex. "I don't know. I haven't convinced you to join me yet. No one's on strike. The article was great, but I don't think it's gonna be that much easier to reach people now."

"Oh, I don't know. Maybe it will be." Alex waited at the top of the hill for Gregory to join him.

"Huh," Gregory said as he got to the top of the hill. "You may be right."

Up ahead, Morris Champlin was spotlit by the morning sun, as always. But unlike normal, there were vans bearing the call letters of five different television stations, a slew of people with TV cameras, and a small handful of reporters waiting at the bottom of the main stairs.

"Is that Principal Macallan peering out from his office?" Alex asked, pointing at a window far away from the crowd.

Gregory rubbed his temples as if it would help him

change the view, but no matter what he did, he could still see his classmates being interviewed, teachers hurrying past reporters, and parents refusing to roll down windows when reporters pushed microphones toward them.

"I should go home," Gregory said suddenly.

"Dude! It's your moment!" Alex started walking forward, then returned to Gregory. "I can also create a distraction if you want to bolt."

"Why are they here? What am I gonna say?" Gregory walked back down the hill a few steps and put his backpack down on the ground and paced fast. "I gotta go home. No, wait. I should go talk to them."

"Take a breath, Gregory K. Take a breath." Alex joined Gregory out of sight from the school. "If you want to talk, you know what to say. Same thing you've been saying. If you want to wait, that's cool too. Just ask yourself which of those makes your calf hurt more."

Gregory stopped moving and took a deep breath. His brow creased in concentration. He shifted his weight from side to side. Alex held his breath.

"Let's go," Gregory said grabbing his backpack. "Change never comes unless somebody speaks up."

Gregory strode off toward the school. Alex gave a celebratory fist pump behind him before catching up.

It didn't take long for someone to recognize Gregory, though when hundreds of schoolmates are milling around and your picture's been in the paper, Gregory figured the odds of someone pointing you out were pretty good regardless. The fact that a dozen reporters and camerapeople hurried over to surround him while he headed toward the school, though, was not expected.

"You're really filming me walk?" Gregory asked a cameraman from Channel 7 Action News.

He never got an answer. The next few minutes were full of shouted questions and brief answers.

"Yes," said Gregory, "I'm still doing all my class work. I plan to pass seventh grade."

"No, I don't think the teachers have it in for me. I like my teachers."

"That's right. I've done no homework at all. The sky did not fall. My test scores didn't fall. My grade did."

"No, that's my brother. I've never won City Math."

Eventually, Gregory found himself two steps up the school staircase with the reporters and fellow students spread out below him. Alex was higher up the staircase, snapping photos. And finally came the question that Gregory had been waiting for—what did he hope to accomplish with his strike?

"These are our lives, and we're not part of this process of figuring out what's acceptable for us. I want that to change. If we need a law protecting us, I want that law," Gregory said. "If we can be part of the process without a law, that's okay too. But even though we're kids, we need to be part of the conversation. There's a town hall meeting coming up here at the school, and I think we should be part of that. Or maybe it's straight to Congress!"

"Good luck with that, Mr. Korenstein-Jasperton. Perhaps I will see you at the next city council meeting if you would like," said a deep voice from the side of the crowd, which Gregory instantly knew was Dr. Bankster. "But for now, I need to get to my classroom, so if you would please disperse your crowd."

There was something about Dr. Bankster that commanded respect, and the crowd of students and reporters parted to let him through. Gregory fell quiet. Dr. Bankster shuffled his way to the stairs and began climbing. He stopped next to Gregory.

"I might as well show you some grading news while we're here, Gregory." Dr. Bankster pulled his grade book out from under his jacket. The cameras were all trained on the duo.

Gregory took a deep breath as Dr. Bankster flipped the book open. He studied the book carefully and shot a quick look at his teacher. Dr. Bankster's gaze did not waver.

"There are consequences for all our actions and for inaction," Dr. Bankster said, closing the book. "I hope that is clear to you."

A reporter shouted out, "Are you passing?"

"That is between Gregory, his parents, the school, and me," Dr. Bankster said fiercely. "Feel free to make your job performance reports public, if you'd like, but this is not a story about one student's grades unless you choose to make it so."

Dr. Bankster turned and walked up the stairs without looking back. Everyone watched as he entered the school, and only then did attention return to Gregory.

"So," another reporter asked, "do you want to tell us if you're passing?"

"No, I don't," Gregory said after a long pause. "I want to tell you that I'm working really hard, and I've promised my parents I'm doing everything I can to pass every class, okay? I just want my voice to be heard."

"Isn't homework part of your job?" another reporter asked.

Gregory grinned. "I don't get paid. And I don't get a voice. I don't think that's fair. No pay? No say? I say no way." Looking out over the crowd of students behind the reporters, Gregory spoke again. "No say? No way! No say? No way!"

As if they'd been waiting for an invitation, the student body answered in kind. "No say? No way! No say? No way!"

The TV cameras swooped around to capture the scene. Hundreds of students stood chanting together, voices raised. Once, twice, ten times . . . and then the morning bell rang. Suddenly, kids were pushing and running and chanting their way up the stairs flooding into Morris Champlin in the final minutes before they'd be reported as late.

Gregory stood in the crowd until he realized that Alex and Ana were gently pushing him to turn and head inside too.

"Nice, GK, nice," she said. "Now don't give Principal Macallan a reason to get you in trouble."

"I think it's a bit late for that," Gregory said.

"Well, no extra reason, dude," Alex said, urging Gregory up.

Just as he disappeared into the school with the crowd, Gregory turned back for a final look at the scene below. The TV cameras were still trained on him and the school doors — reporters were there because of what he was doing. He felt great.

"What did Dr. Bankster show you?" Alex asked. "He was waaaay too many pages into the book to be showing you a grade."

"He showed me a note that said I get two extra credit points if I'm not late for class today."

"What?" Alex asked incredulously.

"I don't have a clue. But I need the points!" And with that Gregory led his friends in a charge up the stairs to Dr. Bankster's room.

They made it with thirty seconds to spare.

Principal Macallan made it to the room with twenty-three seconds to spare. Those seven seconds in between, Gregory realized later, were really great. The rest of the day? It wasn't clear yet, but Gregory knew that the principal was probably not there just for Dr. Bankster's lesson. Macallan was there, no doubt, for him.

12

Alas.
I'm in a class
Where the time just will
not pass.

Ticktock.
It's like a lock
Has been placed upon the clock.

Oh, no.
I wanna go.
Time has never moved so slow.

Bell rings!
What joy that brings.
I can move to other things.

Alas.
Another class.
And the time, again, won't pass.

"Ahh, Principal Macallan," Dr. Bankster said from the front of the room moments after the bell rang, "I am so glad you accepted my invitation to join us today."

"For a minute, I thought I might be the only person who was here on time," Macallan said. Gregory studied his principal's face to see if there was anger or amusement or any emotion he could recognize. All he saw was . . . nothing.

"As you can see, my students know the importance of being on time," Dr. Bankster said, with eyes twinkling. "They also understand the importance of homework, at least based on how many essays I've received about that very topic. I am glad I'll be getting to share them with you."

Macallan rubbed his hands together with anticipation and crossed the room to take a seat Bankster offered near the front. "I don't get nearly enough time in the classroom these days, and homework is one of my favorite things to talk about."

Gregory squirmed and looked around the room to make sure he couldn't accidentally make eye contact with Principal Macallan. Other students, he noticed, were equally squirmy. Elena Todd raised her hand and waited for her teacher to call on her.

"You're not planning on sharing our essays with Principal Macallan, are you?" Elena asked.

"Are you saying, Ms. Todd, that you don't wish your voice to be heard?" Dr. Bankster asked.

"No. I mean. I . . . I thought the paper was for you," Elena's voice faded as she spoke.

"Indeed it is. I promise you that any missing commas, shoddy sentence structure, or particularly choice words will stay between us, as will any brilliant turns of phrase, well-reasoned opinions, or perfectly used semicolons. You may also say whatever you want during this conversation, and it will not impact your essay grade even if it brands you a hypocrite." Dr. Bankster poured himself and Principal Macallan mugs of tea. "As you all know, class participation is a major part of your grade. And so . . . would anyone care to start the conversation today? Homework, yes or no?"

"That's too binary, Dr. Bankster," Ana said without hesitation.

"And to think I was sure that Mr. Korenstein-Jasperton would be the first to speak! But do go on, Ana. Why is that too binary?" Dr. Bankster sipped his tea and waited.

"Some homework could be helpful, so that would be yes. Some homework could just exist to keep us busy, so that would be no. And all homework together is different than one piece alone." Ana finished to silence. And more silence. "Don't leave me hanging here, please."

The same awkward silence returned to the room, with all eyes watching the principal as if he'd magically disappear. After a long pause, Gregory sighed and spoke.

"I think sometimes homework is just pensum, Dr. Bankster. And I don't think that makes it a 'yes.' Do you?" Gregory asked in as friendly a tone as he could.

For a moment, his teacher looked at him, utterly expressionless. Then he cocked his head and laughed. "Yes, yes, that is totally true, Gregory," Bankster said through chuckles. "Well played."

The other students and even Principal Macallan looked confused, as if they wanted to laugh but weren't in on the joke.

"Gregory, would you please explain what *pensum* means, with an obvious example, and how you happened to know this wonderful word?" Bankster sat on the edge of his desk, his giant smile disappearing as he sipped tea.

"A pensum is a piece of schoolwork that is given more as punishment, like, I dunno, an essay on the importance of homework," Gregory said evenly as the class gasped and tittered in unison. "I ran into the word when researching homework conversations through the ages. I confirmed it in a dictionary, which I believe counts as a primary source."

"Indeed it does. Isn't that wonderful, Principal Macallan?" Dr. Bankster said.

"Yes. I suppose it is," the principal agreed.

"Umm, sir? Just so you know, I found that when I was working on my strike," Gregory said. "But it's not why I went on strike."

"Anyone else have something to say about homework's value?" Dr. Bankster asked without acknowledging Gregory's last statement.

Again, there was an awkward silence until finally Benny raised his hand. "Some homework helps me. Some I don't understand. But I do understand that after two hours of working on homework, I am a basket of stress, Dr. Bankster. I don't think that's valuable."

"I see you nodding your head, Ms. Todd,"

Dr. Bankster said as he put down his mug and began to pace. "What are you thinking?"

Gregory could see Elena Todd's shoulders tighten and her finger instinctively twirl her hair as she got put on the spot. He knew that feeling well . . . but he didn't know what Elena would do with it.

"Well, Dr. Bankster, I mean . . ." Elena paused. Everyone held their breath until she expelled hers, exasperated. "We have too much homework. It's ridiculous."

Elena's comment released a tidal wave of conversation, all of which supported Gregory's position. That was no surprise, of course, because who really loved homework?

"It's never helped me anyway," Boris Masterson said. "Like, really, in elementary school, how many multiplication work sheets does it take, you know? Tell me someone's done a study."

"That would be a fine primary source to discover," Dr. Bankster added quickly as the comments flew.

"Homework is for the parents."

"I had to give up band!"

"We can't afford a tutor, so it takes me longer than it takes everyone else."

"It affects our grades, so we have to do it even if we know the material already."

"I used to see the sun!"

"The teachers give it out because they're lazy," said Chuck Dorris. "At least sometimes."

"No," Gregory said before he could stop himself.

"Oh, right. The homework king has spoken," Chuck said.

"Look, we can't know that, and blaming teachers in general doesn't help. They want us to learn, right?" Gregory said.

"No, we're only in it for the money," Dr. Bankster said with a hearty laugh. "I'm curious, Principal Macallan, if you have any comments for the class."

"I've enjoyed the conversation," the principal said carefully. "I do, however, see the value in homework."

"As do I," Dr. Bankster concurred. "What would you say briefly about that?"

"Nothing that will surprise anyone, I'm sure. It reinforces skills. It helps teachers judge what students are learning. It teaches a work ethic. And that's just some of it," Macallan said, rising.

"With due respect, Principal Macallan," Gregory said as his calf began to ache spontaneously, "but do you have any primary sources that prove what you're saying?"

Suddenly, the world slowed down for Gregory, and he became hyperaware of every little detail. In this case, the students' gasps of breath were nearly deafening, the slight hiccup in Bankster's pacing was pronounced, and Principal Macallan's face flashed with anger for just long enough to be noticed before he forced out a smile and laugh that wasn't strong enough to carry to his eyes.

"What was it that Dr. Bankster said before? Well played, Mr. Korenstein-Jasperton," Macallan said as he reached the door. His smile waned. "Come to my office at lunchtime and we will discuss this further."

The click of the door closing echoed through the room, or at least through Gregory's brain. A beat later, he heard a small *dink* as something hit the floor right near him.

"Huh, it really was quiet enough to hear a pen drop," Alex said as he leaned over from his desk and grabbed his pen from the ground.

"Dr. Bankster," Gregory said with rising panic, "was that okay? Did I totally mess up?"

"Primary sources are important, as you know. It

was fair to ask. Your timing may not have been ideal," Bankster acknowledged as he headed to the whiteboard at the front of the room, "but in truth, you were going to end up in the principal's office today no matter what."

"Oh." Gregory slumped in his seat.

"On the plus side, in appreciation for the spirited conversation today"—Dr. Bankster paused and drew a big "no" symbol with red marker on the board—"I will be assigning no homework for the weekend."

A happy murmur ran through the classroom. Dr. Bankster grabbed an eraser and clapped it hard onto the board.

"But don't get used to it." Dr. Bankster vigorously erased the symbol, but Gregory didn't mind. After all, he wasn't doing homework anyway, so it was no reprieve. Which, he had to admit, was kind of ironic since it all happened because of him and his strike.

Still, at the moment, irony was not what he wanted. In fact, what he wanted was a huge hole to open up in the floor that led into a tunnel that would take him to his room.

He didn't get what he wanted and was stuck in class until the bell rang.

"Dude, it's gonna be fine," Alex said as they headed down the stairs after class.

"No. No, it's not." Gregory said. "I appreciate the try, but tell me how it's going to be fine?"

"Because you haven't done anything wrong," Ana said from the stair behind. "Bankster said so."

"Yeah, but Bankster set me up! And anyway, strikes aren't about right or wrong. They're about power. Macallan has the power." Gregory hit the third-floor landing and turned down the hall, heading to math class.

"Gregory K., I'm not sure I agree with you," Benny said, falling into step behind his friend.

"Really, Mr. Banned From Our Group Because Of Macallan's Email?" Gregory's tone was friendly but the impact was still clear.

"That's fear. Not power." Benny stopped at the water fountain in the hall. "I assure you, I know the difference. Please, don't be afraid."

Gregory walked on with Ana and Alex. Ana kept

starting to talk, then biting her lip. Neither boy noticed. Instead, Gregory looked at the floor, and his pace slowed. He shifted his shoulders as if his backpack were getting heavier and heavier . . . the weight of the world bearing down on him.

"You've talked with Macallan before. Nothing's changed." Alex put a hand under Gregory's backpack to support it.

"Except the newspaper story, the TV reporters, and me being a smart-aleck." Gregory leaned against the wall outside his math classroom.

"Yeah, well, when you put it that way . . ." Alex paused before clapping his friend on the back. "You're gonna be fine. I mean, seriously, dude . . . I bet your calf doesn't even hurt."

Gregory closed his eyes and thought it through. All things considered . . . "Yeah. Maybe it's not going to be so bad."

Alex gave an overly big double thumbs-up before heading down the hallway, leaving Gregory alone with Ana.

"He didn't set you up," Ana said. Gregory looked at her blankly. "Dr. Bankster. I don't know what he did, but it wasn't a setup."

"Felt like it," Gregory muttered, plopping his backpack on the floor.

"He's not like that," Ana said. "So there's something you're missing."

"Why are you defending him? He gives you so much homework it makes your eyes swim," Gregory said.

"And he helps me with it, more than any other teacher," Ana said simply. "I'm dyslexic, Gregory K. Reading and writing exhaust me. I told Dr. Bankster, and he's given me recorded versions of every piece of reading this year. Sometimes it's books on tape, and sometimes it's him reading the stuff and putting it on a thumb drive for me, okay? He's had me skip a lot of essays and do spoken reports for him. He's tough, but he's not setting you up."

"That's why you're at his office hours." Gregory stated it, not asked it. "I had no idea you were dyslexic."

"Yeah, well. I don't talk about it." Ana's voice had the lightness of relief to it. "And I don't have a big D printed on me."

"No. That's my report card." Gregory grinned. "Thanks, Ana. For . . . you know. I mean . . . I hear you."

"You're welcome. It wasn't a setup. And I agree with Benny: Don't be afraid. Macallan won't be so bad." Ana lifted Gregory's backpack and handed it to him. "Now, we've got class."

Gregory held on to the idea that it wasn't going to be so bad all the way through math class and right up until lunchtime, when he headed to Principal Macallan's office. The door was closed, but the secretary had told him to knock, so he did.

The principal opened the door with a thin smile. "Gregory, Gregory, Gregory. Do come in."

Gregory had taken one step in when realized that, in fact, it probably was going to be so bad. Or maybe worse. "Mom? Dad? What are you doing here?"

The principal's office wasn't big to begin with, but with his mom and dad already inside, there didn't seem to be room to breathe. The family members acknowledged each other with looks and smiles . . . though not happy ones.

"I called your parents in," the principal said, though Gregory had figured that it was unlikely his parents both happened to be coming by to visit. "Why don't we all sit down?"

Three chairs were opposite Macallan's desk, and his parents took the ones on the outsides. There'd be no quick getaway, Gregory knew, as he sat between his mom and dad.

"There's much to discuss today," Principal Macallan said as he went behind his desk, "and none of you will be surprised to know that it's all related to Gregory's so-called homework strike."

Furrowing his brow and gripping his chair's arms, Gregory managed not to respond to what sounded like a huge slight.

"Did you see the newspaper this morning, Principal Macallan? It was nice for us to see Gregory in the pages instead of O," Mom said.

"I have seen the paper, yes. I have seen the news vans too."

"News vans," Dad said flatly. "I see."

"Gregory's efforts have become a huge distraction for us here at Morris Champlin. Our students are losing time from their studies," Macallan continued, "and a few of them have stopped turning in homework."

"Really?" Gregory couldn't help himself. He smiled.

"Unfortunately so. Our teachers are struggling. The news vans today mean more attention and time spent on this issue." Macallan took a deep breath. "Your strike is impacting the education of your peers, Gregory. It needs to stop."

"Well . . ." Gregory started, but Macallan cut him off.

"Your strike is also affecting your ability to pass your classes," Macallan said, grabbing a paper-clipped pile of papers from his desk and handing it to Gregory's mom. "As you can see from the printouts, Gregory's grades are sliding. He is in danger of failing seventh grade."

His mother tutted — there was no other word for it — as she reviewed the papers. "Principal Macallan, you know we're also focused on Gregory passing his classes."

"Of course," the principal replied.

"And we don't want him to be a distraction to the work you're doing here. But . . . well . . . he hasn't been rude or disrespectful, has he?" His mother finished looking at the papers and handed them over to his dad.

"Many teachers are feeling rather disrespected, I'm afraid." Macallan wrung his hands.

"But, Principal Macallan . . . I've never said a bad word about any of them. I don't complain. I like my teachers!" Gregory said.

"Your actions, however, create a different vibe. You're responsible for that."

"I'm responsible for how the teachers feel? Wait a second . . ." Gregory's face burned, though he wasn't sure if it was red or not.

"Gregory," his mom interrupted. "Principal Macallan, if I can try to rephrase that a little . . ."

"No, Mom. This is important. I had three hours of homework a day. The teachers gave that homework. My actions come from their actions!" Gregory grabbed the chair to keep from leaping out. "I'm expressing my feelings. I would think all of you would support that. I'd think you'd turn next week's town hall meeting into a whole night on homework, and I'd think you'd want to hear us students out."

"You heard your classmates today, Gregory. The disrespect is growing because of your actions. And even more to the point, you have a report card full of

Cs and Ds that are threatening to slide into Fs. Tell me that's what you really want." The principal looked calmly at Gregory, but there was no calm to stare back with.

"These grades are very interesting," his father said quietly.

"They are very poor," the principal added. "And it hurts me to see."

"Numbers are fascinating to me," Gregory's father said, "as you can look at them in different ways. Clearly, Gregory's overall grades are sliding as he's been on strike."

"They are, indeed," the principal echoed.

"But if you actually look at his test grades, they are trending up. His in-class participation grades, too." Dad put the papers back on Macallan's desk and pointed to a few different areas. "It's fascinating, actually, that if it were tests and participation alone, he'd be getting As and Bs in all his classes."

"Yes, well, it's not tests and participation alone," Macallan said.

"But why is that?" Dad asked, and Gregory's jaw fell open. "I mean, isn't the goal of any class to teach the material? And doesn't passing tests show you know the material?"

"It's not that simple," Macallan sputtered.

"But it could be that simple. And I'm not sure I understand why it isn't." His father's eyes looked at some point far above Macallan's shoulder. Gregory knew his dad was playing with numbers in his head, though what those numbers might mean, he couldn't possibly guess.

"This meeting is not about philosophy, Mr. Korenstein-Jasperton," Macallan said with far too much butter in his voice. "What I am trying to express is that there are many reasons why it would benefit your son to get out of the public eye, return to his studies, and give up his strike."

Gregory reached down and put his hand on his calf, testing the waters. "I don't want to be rude, but I don't see the reasons. I see reasons you want me to stop. But that's different."

Macallan slapped his hand down on the table, and while it sounded angry to Gregory, the principal's smile never left his face. "I am hopeful that your parents will be able to explain to you the importance of making a sound decision here. For your grades. For the school. For your future."

Macallan stood up, his imposing presence making all three Korenstein-Jaspertons shrink back a little.

"I am happy to answer any questions you might have," Macallan continued. "This is important, so I'll make time."

Ten minutes later, Gregory left Macallan's office and paced in the hallway outside it. Ten minutes after that, his mom and dad left the principal's office, and they all walked through the maze of hallways leading out.

"Is there anything we could say to get you to stop your strike right now?" his father asked when they could tell Macallan was out of earshot.

"Gregory . . . I . . ." His mother trailed off, unable to find the words.

"Did either of you see or hear anything in there that makes you think I absolutely have to stop now? That I should stop now?" Gregory asked after a brief pause.

His father chuckled. "You remind me of your mother, Gregory K."

"You have to pass your classes," his mother said as she slipped her hand into his father's hand.

"I am!" Gregory's exasperation could barely contain itself.

"Good," his mom said quietly. "It's not going to get easier."

"I know."

"And you should definitely not stop now," his mother whispered. Then she took a deep breath and spoke quite loudly, in case anyone was able to hear them. "I'm very proud of you."

His parents said nothing else, but his mom reached out with her free hand and grabbed his hand. Gregory gratefully squeezed back. He might be fighting the system . . . but it sure was nice to have his parents on his side.

And if they simply had a magic wand to wave to make all his problems go away, that would make it better.

But they didn't. And he didn't.

And as the day went on, the problems didn't go away. In fact, to Gregory . . . they felt like they were getting worse every single minute.

13

When a group has a problem, unite to defeat it.

Don't try to solve all your problems alone:

Study your history, or else you'll repeat it.

Whatever the issue, you rise up to meet it—

Look for solutions, don't sit back and moan.

When a group has a problem, unite to defeat it.

When you take an action, you cannot delete it.

Move forward, accepting mistakes as your own.

Study your history, or else you'll repeat it.

The hard work must happen. There's no way to cheat it.

Shortcuts won't help you, but pathways are known:

When a group has a problem, unite to defeat it.

The status quo is, unless you unseat it.

From your days as a child until you are grown

Study your history, or else you'll repeat it.

The task may be huge, but you can complete it.

Your fears and your worries are all overblown.

When a group has a problem, unite to defeat it.

Study your history, or else you'll repeat it.

The best part of most school days was the final bell, at least for Gregory and his friends, and today was definitely no exception. Ever since his lunch meeting, Gregory had been breathless, feeling trapped and overwhelmed. As he burst out of the building with Ana, Alex, and Benny, the sun and fresh air washed over him, his shoulders unhunched, and his breathing slowly returned to normal.

"Your parents were totally cool with everything, right?" Ana asked as they fled down the front stairs of the school.

"They were awesome. But it's not over, you know?" Gregory said. "Macallan . . . he . . . he isn't happy, and the thing he isn't happy with is all because of me."

"He can't kick you out of school, dude," Alex chimed in while busily trying to zip closed the multiple pockets on his backpack. "I don't think."

"Yeah, but my dad did the math. My test scores are getting better, but math and Spanish are looking like Ds and history is gonna be hard to pass if nothing changes. And what's gonna change? I mean, fast enough to matter?" Gregory's voice was firm, not whiny. "And I'm tired."

"It was only this morning, Gregory K.," Benny said,

"that you were a TV star smiling as though he owned the world."

"What a difference a day at school makes," Gregory replied.

"Enjoy your weekend, everyone," Benny said as he zigged right while the rest of the group zigged left. "It's time for me to be far away from you evil influences."

Ana, Gregory, and Alex watched Benny head away. "You aren't evil, Gregory," Ana said.

"Nah, but evil comes from him," Alex added. "Eviiiiillllll."

"So, you guys wanna come over and watch me be evil on the news?" Gregory asked. "Assuming I made it on."

"I'm so in," Ana said, "I won't even bring my homework."

"Evil," Gregory laughed. "You're evil!"

In light of the special occasion, Gregory's mom decided not to cook and ordered pizza instead. The whole family, including O, piled into the living room, pizza boxes in tow. Ana and Alex joined Gregory on the floor in front of the couch. The TV at the front of the room played the local news, and a picture-in-picture window on the TV showed a second channel.

"Did you say channels five and seven were both there?" his mom asked.

"Every channel was there, Mrs. Korenstein-Jasperton," Alex said. "It was like the end of City Math, only with more excitement."

O shrugged. "It's all relative."

"Are we recording?" Mom asked. Gregory's dad nodded.

"Indeed we are. And I have friends from work recording every channel too, just to make sure," he added.

"You know, it's not that big a deal," Gregory said from the floor.

"Yeah, you're right. You've been on TV every week since I moved here," Ana said.

"I think a poetry-writing reality show would be great television," Kay said as she reached over and stole a piece of Gregory's pizza from his plate. "Seriously, the drama of waiting to see if a poet has picked a perfect word . . ."

All eyes were on Kay and none of them looked in agreement.

"You have no vision, people." Kay gobbled her pilfered slice. "No vision."

"Do they show everything they film each day?" Gregory asked suddenly. "What if I don't make it?"

"My phone started ringing this afternoon when a Channel 7 announcer said 'tonight on the six o'clock news, we'll talk to a local boy who's gone on a homework strike,' so I think your vanity can disappear," O said. "As can your pepperoni."

O grabbed another slice of pizza from his brother's plate, but Gregory didn't care. His stomach was dancing, and all he focused on was breathing. Conversation continued among family and friends as the news began, but Gregory was barely aware of it, even when his brother-sense tingled and told him O was insulting him.

Finally, with short screams and loud shushes filling the room, the story came on Channel 7.

Most of the report was a blur to Gregory. The reporter framed the story about homework and a "local boy who wants his voice to be heard." There were shots of Morris Champlin, Gregory speaking from the steps — "These are our lives, and we're not part of this process of figuring out what's acceptable for us.

I want that to change. If we need a law protecting us, I want that law"—and a shot of the crowd of students in support.

"That's me!" Ana said when she saw herself chanting on screen. Alex gave her a high five across Kay, who'd settled between them.

One part Gregory hadn't seen before was Principal Macallan standing in front of the school trophy case, looking totally calm under the camera's bright lights. "Homework is a part of school here, and like every part of the educational plan we've created for our students, great thought and care is given to how it's used. Everything we do is focused on helping each of our students reach their maximum potential, and sometimes, just like it was for me and probably for you, it can feel a little overwhelming. That's just a natural part of growing up . . . and even of being an adult."

Finally, the reporter turned to the camera, Morris Champlin framed behind her. "There is tremendous passion here among the student body. As one student, who asked not to be identified, told me, homework is the biggest source of stress between him and his parents, him and his teachers, and him and his friends. Otherwise, he has no problems with it. Still, despite that attitude, we are unaware of any other student who has joined Gregory Korenstein-Jasperton on his homework strike. The risk, apparently, remains too great, although as young Gregory said today, isn't learning the real goal? Sometimes it does not seem that way."

The living room erupted into applause, with even O giving a few polite claps.

"You were totally awesome," Ana said, leaning over and giving Gregory a sort-of-sideways high five.

"It was all right," Gregory said, though his grin was way bigger than all right.

"No one has joined you?" O asked. "My brother has NO followers? I'm . . . I'm . . ."

"Can it, O," Kay interrupted, the only person with such authority. "That will change."

Gregory's mom began gathering up dirty pizza plates. His dad rose to help.

"I wonder, Gregory," Dad said while he grabbed a glass from the floor, "when was the last time you simply asked people directly to go on strike with you? Not to have their voice heard, but to actually strike."

"Oh, come on, Dad!" Gregory sounded annoyed. "I've asked . . . I mean, I . . . huh."

"Yes?" Dad's tone showed his grin.

"It's been a while," Gregory admitted.

"Reinforce the message, Gregory. Over and over and over, if you have to," his mother said. "I mean, that's just a suggestion."

"And now you've got momentum, dude!" Alex crawled across the floor to the chair vacated by Gregory's dad and climbed in, stretching out his legs gratefully.

"My grade can't take it," Ana shrugged. "The strike could go on for months."

"But could your grades take a week?" Gregory asked.

"Exactly what I was thinking!" Kay said. "Like a one-week walkout versus everyone staying forever on a picket line."

"So, if homework makes up twenty percent of my grade, and I skip one week . . ." Ana scrunched her forehead.

"A half a percent," O said quickly.

"Assuming forty weeks of school, with each week having the same amount of homework assignments, of course," Kay added.

"About five-eighths if it's twenty-five percent of your grade," Dad added as he left the room.

"Or three-quarters of a percent for thirty percent," Gregory's mom shouted from somewhere out in the hall.

"Is it always like this around here?" Ana asked.

"You mean where Gregory fails to do math like the rest of us? Yes," O said, getting up from his seat, "that's usually what it's like around here before breakfast is even over. Now, if you'll excuse me, I have better things to do than watch TV. Although I will say, Gregory K., that you did okay, and I thank you for not embarrassing me."

O left the room. Gregory and Kay looked at each other, mouths hung open.

"Your brother can be . . ." Ana stopped herself.

"That was the highest praise ever," Gregory said. "I really must've been good on TV."

"I'll say," Kay said.

"Dudes and dudettes, can we return to Gregory K.'s plan? This strike ain't gonna strike itself, ya know." Alex reached into his pocket and pulled out his cell phone. "Boy, this thing has been vibrating since the news."

"Mine too," Ana said. "Texts and every social network I'm on. Everyone's talking about you."

"We need to talk back," Gregory said, jumping to his feet. "We need a one-week homework strike so that Macallan takes us seriously."

"Hard to sell," Ana said. "Sorry."

"Then what isn't hard to sell?" Gregory asked, frustrated. "I mean, I've been on strike for weeks now, and I'm still passing. I just take it day by day and . . ."

"Bingo! Winner!" Kay said.

"One day?" Gregory asked.

"One day," Ana agreed.

"One little day. That's like point-one percent of a grade," Alex added. "No one will even notice."

"But maybe everyone will notice," Gregory said. "It's worth a shot, anyway. Show 'em we can do it, then see what happens. Maybe it'll become sticky." Gregory eyed his friends. "You guys gonna help?"

"Oh, you know it," Ana said, warming up her texting fingers. "Let's get this rolling."

Alex nervously bounced his leg up and down over and over. He said nothing.

"Alex," Gregory said. "I know you're a reporter and all . . ."

"I just don't know if I'll join you," Alex said softly after a pause.

"Dude," Ana said, "I know homework's pretty easy for you and all, but seriously! One day?"

"It's not that simple," Alex said. "If it were that simple, everyone would be on strike."

"It's that simple now," Ana said. "At least for me."

"But that's because you finally admitted that you missed painting, Ana," Gregory said. "Being busy is good, but it makes it so you don't really think about what you're missing. And when you realize it, it's even harder to accept it. I know it wasn't easy for me. I felt stupid and powerless."

There was a long, quiet moment. "Alex," Gregory said, breaking the silence. "I miss the movies you used to make. I miss hearing about all the new graphic novels you read, since now you're not reading them. But I love that you've taken the newspaper and run with it and keep up with all your tutoring too. And I would love your help organizing Monday's strike, okay? Seriously. That would be amazing."

"I'll help organize," Alex agreed after a few moments. "I mean, I have to answer all these texts anyway."

"Awesome. No Homework Monday, here we come!" Gregory said.

As his friends began to text and type on their

phones, Gregory realized he wasn't going to be much use in organizing. He'd go out over the weekend and see who he could talk to, sure, but he wasn't connected online or off. Still, it didn't take long for Ana and Alex to get replies — folks were totally in for a one-day strike. And Gregory knew that they'd enjoy it. And from there? Well, the sky was the limit.

Word spread faster than Gregory's parents' friends' phone calls arrived. The whole evening consisted of phones ringing and vibrating. Maybe watching the local news on a Friday night wasn't the most fun you could have, but it definitely was something that people did. Friends and relatives called to talk with Gregory and his family. Classmates buzzed, literally, on Ana's and Alex's phones and figuratively in conversation.

A group of five eighth graders Gregory didn't even know came by the house just to say "awesome!" and agreed on the spot to a one-day homework strike with "details to come."

By the time Ana and Alex left for home, over half the middle school had heard about the upcoming action, and almost all of them had agreed. Even Benny sent word through a neutral party that he was "all in." The plan was simple — always be polite and respectful to the teachers, but simply leave all homework assignments in the classroom. If there was reading, don't do it. If there was writing, leave the page blank.

And most important, everyone was to spend the afternoon time doing something that they loved doing but no longer felt they had enough time to do.

"Unless you're grounded," Alex added helpfully. "Then . . . oh well."

It was around nine p.m. when Gregory realized he was utterly exhausted. He spoke quickly with his Aunt Muriel, who had called from New Jersey, then headed down to his room for one final phone call.

Kelly answered before the first ring had finished. "You were fantastic! We watched it on the computer down here. My mom says you made her proud."

"Like 'I'll send you a pie' proud or just an adult saying proud?" Gregory asked as he flopped on his bed.

"Pies. Many pies," Kelly replied. "So now what?"

Gregory filled her in on the one-day plan, and his calf didn't hurt once.

"What if I wanted to do it too?" Kelly finally asked.

"I figured after you moved, you didn't have to be part of any of my crazy plans," Gregory said.

"I don't. But this one's not crazy. So I'd need instructions. A bunch of guidelines." Kelly's fingers clicking on a keyboard came through over the phone. "Is Kay still up?"

"Uhh, yeah. Why?" Gregory's voice rose with confusion.

"Well, unless you've started building websites, I have a project for her. And do you know anyone who can do some graphics?" Kelly was calm, directed, efficient, and leaving Gregory in total silence. After a beat, she spoke again. "Right. I've lost you. My bad. Gregory, you need to get online."

"Online?" Gregory hopped up and walked over to his desk.

"Yep. Happy birthday. My mom and I just bought you homeworkstrike-dot-com." Kelly's unseen fingers clickety-clacked away. "Now start writing up some instructions."

"Instructions for how you could organize a strike?" Gregory grabbed a notebook and flipped it open.

"Not just me, Gregory K. Anyone!" Kelly whooped a little, and Gregory's eyes sparked back to life, the tiredness replaced by laser focus . . . or at least the hope of apple pie. "Now get me Kay!"

An hour later, Kay and Kelly had put together the bare bones of a website. Ana had begun working on some graphics while she and Alex continued to coordinate the Monday strike action at Morris Champlin. And Gregory had written instructions, slogans, and a poem or two just for fun.

The energy flowed right up until Gregory collapsed into bed, drained from the adrenaline rush of the day. TV, a website, and thirteen different relatives was enough for anyone . . . and he only hoped tomorrow would be a much mellower day.

Saturdays had always been Gregory's favorite day of the week. They tended to be pretty fun and came with the added bonus of one more weekend day after. He loved to sleep in and laze around whenever he could.

This particular Saturday, he couldn't.

"Out of curiosity," his mom said while knocking on his door at eight a.m., "would you be more interested in talking to the *New York Times*, CNN, or Principal Macallan to start your day?"

Gregory pulled the pillow over his head and shouted out a muffled "Can I say 'none of the above'?"

"You can. But your dad and I have to talk to your principal." His mom's voice stopped, but Gregory heard no retreating footsteps. After a long pause, he lifted the pillow back up.

"What is it?" Gregory said to the door.

"Well . . . Gregory . . . we just . . . it's only . . ." His mom took a deep breath. "I'll make you some breakfast if you want to come up. It's a big day. You gotta eat."

Twenty minutes later, Gregory had eaten his fill of bacon without having to fend off O or any reporters. The phone had rung three times as they ate, but his parents were sending everything to voice mail now.

And decisions had been made.

"No newspaper interviews. No TV. Nothing until there's actual news that isn't just a story about me," Gregory repeated to make it real in his head. "I've been heard enough."

"And if someone wants to do a story?" Dad asked.

"Tell them I'm busy not doing my homework!" Gregory pushed away from the table, grabbed his dishes, and walked over to give his mom a kiss and his dad a shoulder bump. "Thanks for not grounding me."

"Well," his mother said with a smile, "the weekend isn't over yet!"

The weekend wasn't over, but Gregory knew it would be soon enough. So he decided to enjoy every minute of it he could.

He grabbed a notebook and went to write at the Slice. He finished two poems, polished a short story, and even wrote a free-form journal entry about his experiences with the strike. Having something to focus on made the time fly.

He met up with Alex and Ana and a few other classmates for a game of Ultimate Frisbee.

He called Kelly and walked through the city park while they spoke.

He waved to lots of fellow students, got the cold shoulder from some, noticed that quite a few parents were glaring his way, and even signed a few autographs. Sure, he'd dreamed of signing his own books someday, but signing his picture in the newspaper wasn't a bad thing either.

Gregory went to bed early on Sunday, totally exhausted and unsure what Monday would bring.

Well, he knew it would be another day of him not doing homework, but would he be alone again? Or would the plan everyone was talking about actually happen? And was his plan even a good idea?

As he drifted off, Gregory focused on his calf. It didn't hurt.

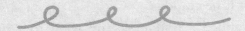

The next morning, Gregory met Alex and Ana for the walk to school. He was calm, and they were nearly bubbling out of their shoes. At school, there were smiles and furtive eye contact but not much was said to Gregory. Or maybe he just didn't hear it as he hurried up to Dr. Bankster's room to start the day.

There was a lesson in class, but Gregory wasn't really able to engage. All he knew was that it was taking an incredibly long time.

Finally, Dr. Bankster finished whatever it was he was saying and walked about the room handing out the day's homework. The teacher paused dramatically by Gregory, offering the sheet to his student . . . but Gregory declined.

As he did every class, Bankster returned to the front of the room. "Any final thoughts today?"

There was a tiny pause, then Gregory and Ana rose to their feet with the whole class a half second behind.

"No homework without representation!" they all shouted in unison. "No say? No way! No say? No way!"

The school bell rang, and Gregory's classmates filed out of the room, still chanting. On each desk, the homework sheets stayed behind, in a statement of unity. Gregory scanned until he found Alex, still near his desk, hands on his homework. At the last moment, Alex turned and followed the crowd, leaving the single white paper behind. Gregory couldn't contain his smile.

As the chanting faded in the distance, Gregory watched Dr. Bankster staring impassively . . . and then slowly going around the room collecting the papers.

Now Gregory stood stock-still, the only student remaining.

"You're going to be late, Gregory K.," Bankster said without turning around. "You should go."

"At least this time it was a group of allies, Dr. Bankster." Gregory slowly gathered his belongings. "I'm not gonna lose three more points, am I?"

"Not for this, no." Dr. Bankster turned around,

grinned, and raised a single bushy eyebrow. "But I don't teach all your classes. Now go!"

Relieved by the smile and the news about the three points, Gregory finished gathering his stuff and hurried off.

As soon as he hit the third-floor hallway, Gregory knew this wasn't going to be a day like any other. Students were high-fiving one another, and he overheard snippets of conversation letting him know that he was not alone. There was a homework strike for real.

And if he questioned that even a little, he didn't when he saw Principal Macallan in the hall between second and third periods . . . or again when he was summoned to his office in the middle of the next class.

"You really don't give up, do you?" Principal Macallan seemed even bigger today . . . or his office had shrunk. Gregory sat in the chair opposite Macallan's desk, feeling small.

"I am on strike, sir. That's all," Gregory said.

"I am unhappy with this disrespectful display today." Macallan drummed his fingers on his desk.

"Disrespectful?" Gregory asked.

"Yes. That's one word I'd use," Macallan said.

"Really?" Gregory said. He knew he shouldn't get angry in the principal's office, but he couldn't help it. "It's not just me today. It's everyone, so don't blame me. And if there's any disrespect here, it's that you are not listening to what we're saying. Sir. Principal Macallan. Uh . . . sir."

"I hear what you're saying. I just don't agree with it, Mr. Korenstein-Jasperton." Principal Macallan sighed heavily. "I don't want Morris Champlin on the news again. More specifically, I don't want to be on the news."

"Me neither," Gregory said honestly.

"There is the town hall meeting on Wednesday evening. We have a lot to discuss, but I will give you time to make your case, if you would like, along with other teachers and administrators." Macallan's tight smile made Gregory speak quickly.

"Absolutely. I'd love that." Gregory knew he had to end the meeting now even though it wasn't really up to him. "Can I get back to class now? I really can't afford to lower my participation grade, you know?"

Macallan laughed despite himself. "Go. And let's try to keep this low-key, okay?"

"I promise I'll only tell my closest friends," Gregory said as he hurried out of the room.

"Doomed!" Macallan said as Gregory disappeared. "We're doomed!"

Gregory wasn't sure if that was a joke or not, but he decided not to go back and check. He'd gotten exactly what he'd wanted.

It was a huge opportunity.

He just hoped he didn't blow it.

Yell.

Shout!

Be proud.

Let it out.

Speak aloud each word:

Yes, I want my voice to be heard!

14

By the end of the day, almost everybody in town knew the news. And everyone had advice for Gregory too — everything from not giving in to the powers that be to suggesting he apologize for being such a disgrace. Adults, in particular, stared and looked disappointed.

"There's a lot of anger," Ana said as they walked home from school that day.

"I think I'll hide in my room and write," Gregory replied.

Hiding wasn't entirely possible. His parents screened calls from newspapers and TV stations. He answered email questions from his friends. He refused to weigh in on whether the other kids should continue their strike, though momentum after one day was pretty strong for more of the same.

"I played basketball all afternoon!" Gregory heard from one classmate. "I slept!" and "I played video games!" and "I'm not sure what I did, but it was really great" were a few of the other emails he got. And Alex came by to show Gregory a short film he'd started.

"I missed this. Like, a lot," Alex said.

"Me too," Gregory said before offering a few story ideas.

Not everyone was pleased, though, as visible counter-protests — or, as Alex said, "There are pro-homework rallies!" — greeted him at school the next morning.

Somehow, mostly by hiding behind his friends and staying in his room, Gregory got through the next two days. He worked on his own manuscript. He worked on what he would say at the town hall meeting. He worked incredibly hard on everything related to school except homework. And for a couple of days, the same was true of most of his classmates — the strike was sticky.

Finally, Wednesday evening rolled around, and from Gregory's perspective, it couldn't have come sooner. Or later, really, when he thought about it. It was simply inevitable . . . and finally here.

As Gregory, Kay, and his parents arrived at the school, a huge throng of supporters erupted in cheers. Right nearby, a smaller—though certainly not small—group of parents and kids stood holding HOMEWORK MATTERS! and SUPPORT THE TEACHERS! signs.

"I support the teachers," Gregory muttered to his parents. They said nothing, just held their smiles in place and gently urged Gregory forward.

A chant of "No Strike!" rose from the hardy band of sign carriers. The rest of the crowd chanted "No say? No way!" right back at them.

"How can you tell which group is the protestors," Kay wondered, "when both sides are chanting?"

Gregory and his family climbed the stairs and went inside the school. The auditorium was already jam-packed, but there was a row of reserved seats right up front for those who were speaking during the meeting. And, in the case of Gregory, seats for his mother, father, and Kay too.

The room was buzzing, but Gregory sat down and tried to zone out.

Most of the time, school meetings were boring affairs. Sure, there was great information given out and parents loved the chance to meet the people who worked with their kids for hours a day . . . but it was rare that people shouted, held up banners, or brought their children. It was also rare for there to be TV cameras—actually, according to Gregory's dad, it wasn't rare but unprecedented—but there they were.

"Gregory," his mother said softly, "don't forget to breathe."

It was sound advice, and Gregory knew he'd need to keep hearing it all night long.

Eventually, the town hall meeting started. Principal Macallan stood behind a lectern on the stage of the auditorium, five empty chairs to one side of him. He introduced himself and did some housekeeping about upcoming days off and the like. But no one was really listening, and he knew it.

"Right. So. Tonight we wish to give part of the meeting over to a conversation about homework in our school. As many of you, or probably all of you, know, one of our students, Gregory Korenstein-Jasperton, has been on a homework strike for some time. It was a small act of civil disobedience practiced by him alone. This week, however, a large number of other students joined in." Principal Macallan paused as a few supportive shouts erupted. He held up his hand to quiet the voices.

"Tonight we have come together to have a respectful conversation about the issues," the principal continued, grabbing the mic from its holder and pacing the front of the stage. "While we as a school support our students' rights to express themselves, we also have a clear focus on education. My fellow administrators and teachers here at Morris Champlin are highly trained, highly experienced, and totally dedicated to helping our students achieve their potential. Over the summer, each teacher prepares a syllabus for his or her class. They know what they have to teach, and they figure out the best way to teach it. They are conscious of the demands on their students, as well as what others in the world expect of our students later in life. I want you to hear from some of these people tonight."

Gregory watched as four adults walked onto the stage from the wings—his math teacher; an English teacher and the vice principal, whom he didn't know; and

Dr. Bankster. The four walked across the stage and sat in the empty seats, leaving only one open. Gregory took a very deep breath, quickly grabbed his mother and father's hands, and waited.

"We've also invited Gregory to join us onstage so we can all hear the various points of view," Principal Macallan said, returning to the lectern. "So, if you'd join us . . ."

Hoots and applause drowned out whatever final thought the principal might have had. Gregory rose from his chair and climbed the stairs on the side of the stage. He tried to smile and tried even harder not to trip. He took the only open seat, right next to Dr. Bankster, and looked out at the crowd.

He'd been in this auditorium a few times this school year already, as well as for various events over the years. It looked totally different from the stage. From up here, he could feel the lights burning down on him, see the hundreds of people looking up at him, and hear the breathing and mumbling from the crowd as well as every squeaky chair in the whole old room. Sweat began to trickle down his neck, and he thought his right hand was twitching.

He caught sight of Ana and her father about a third

of the way back. He could see Alex in the press section near the front. And then, just as Macallan started to speak again, he saw the doors at the back of the room open up and Kelly and her mom step inside. Gregory immediately checked in with himself—his calf didn't hurt. Suddenly, he was as relaxed as could be.

The first four speakers, including Principal Macallan, said nothing that surprised Gregory—homework reinforces learning; it teaches responsibility; it allows more material to be covered; it helps teachers see where students are. The goal, as was often repeated, was not to overwhelm anyone. In fact, no teacher gives that much homework.

Gregory had heard it all before, and it was still all true too, but beside the point. He waited until the vice principal finished up, and then it was his turn. Dr. Bankster would have the final word of the conversation this evening. Gregory figured that was better than Macallan ending things . . . though maybe not much.

Principal Macallan introduced Gregory, asked the audience to remain respectful and quiet, then moved aside as Gregory stood behind the lectern.

"Thank you, Principal Macallan." Gregory's voice

coming out of the speakers made him do a little double take. "And thank you to all the teachers and parents and everyone who has come out tonight. I want to say again that I like all my teachers this year. I am not mad at them. I think teachers are on our side and have a really hard job to do, and I'm really glad they do it."

A round of applause caused Gregory to pause. He waited for the clapping to slow. "The thing is, this isn't about the teachers. This is about us, the students." Applause and hooting filled the auditorium, but this time Gregory didn't wait long to continue. "We're all different. What takes me fifteen minutes to do for English homework takes my friend Ana forty-five. What takes my friend Benny five minutes to do in math takes me an hour. Homework adds up. I was doing three hours a day, and sometimes I still didn't get it all done. And what was I giving up? Everything else. Everything that means something to me beyond school."

Gregory uncoupled the mic from the stand and moved to the front of the stage. "And you know what I've learned since I've been on strike? I can pass tests without doing my homework. I pass them because I want to learn. I work hard. Really hard. And I still get to do the things I didn't have time for before. My test grades have gone up, not because I got smarter or the teachers got better or because I put in more time. It's because I'm making the choices. It's because I'm giving myself choices."

Again, hoots and hollers filled the hall, but this time there were a few jeers too. "You're just a kid!" an adult's voice rang out. "There are rules!" another voice cried.

"I'm here today because I want my voice to be heard. I want to be part of the conversation about what I do outside of school. I know there's all sorts of research and studies to point to and no one has bad intentions, but I know the homework situation wasn't working for me. I didn't go on strike to be disrespectful. I went on strike to show myself respect." Gregory paused again as applause and boos mixed together. "Principal Macallan, I don't know the solution. I just know that the way things are going now can't keep going. Maybe there needs to be a law again. And since no one seems willing to listen, then that's why we have to keep speaking up. I just know that we students need to be included in the conversations and solutions. We don't get a say in what happens. And right now, by our actions, we're telling you no say, no way."

This time, the applause drowned out any boos. Gregory tried to fight off a smile, but he couldn't do it. He hurried back to the lectern and put the mic away before collapsing back in his seat.

Dr. Bankster slowly rose from his chair, and a wave of quiet rolled over the crowd. By the time he'd taken the ten steps to the podium, the auditorium had fallen silent.

What was it, Gregory wondered, that gave his teacher such power? Whatever it was, Gregory vowed that when he grew up, he'd have it too. He watched Bankster adjust the microphone. Gregory tried to swallow, but his mouth was totally dry. This was the big moment, and now all he could do was listen.

"You should truly be ashamed," Dr. Bankster began. Gregory shifted miserably in his seat and cast his eyes over at his teacher. Bankster's gaze locked onto him. "No, not you, Gregory. Anyone here who has tried to shout you down should be ashamed. Anyone here who has not listened to what you have been saying should be embarrassed."

Stunned in his seat, Gregory mouthed a "thank you" to Dr. Bankster. The crowd remained nearly silent.

"The work this young man has done has been truly impressive," Dr. Bankster continued, sucking in the attention of everyone in the room, "and in all my years of teaching—and let's be honest: I've taught almost everyone in this room because I've been teaching a lot of years—his determination and methods have been the most impressive I have seen. It has been a privilege watching."

A few hoots and whistles reached the stage, and Gregory could see his parents beaming.

"Decades ago, I went before our city council to ask them about the same law that Gregory Korenstein-Jasperton discovered not long ago, a law that banned homework for those under the age of fifteen. I asked the council if that law was still on the books, and if so, why wasn't it being enforced? At that meeting, they began the process of removing the law from the city regulations. It was never enforced. At the time, I was outraged. I wanted that law more than anything."

"No way!" was shouted from somewhere deep in the crowd. Nervous laughter agreed with the sentiment.

"I know you're surprised. And, Gregory?" Dr. Bankster looked at his student with a smile. "I was one primary source you never checked out."

The teachers onstage laughed right along with Gregory.

"Years have passed since then, and I have changed in many ways. And I am sorry to tell you that I no longer believe there should be a law banning homework. So while I am exceedingly impressed with you, Gregory, I am in disagreement with your goals. Teachers need every tool available to them, and a ban on one such tool helps no one." Dr. Bankster paused for a sip of water.

Alone in his chair, Gregory felt drops of sweat on his neck again and knew his ears were turning red. He was sure he was shrinking in the bright lights and under the pressure of Dr. Bankster's words being shared in front of everyone. All of a sudden, the last place he wanted to be was onstage. He looked out into the crowd, hoping to see Kelly to bolster him, but the lights in his eyes made it hard to find her. Dr. Bankster's pause seemed interminable, but eventually, he spoke again.

"That said, it was also not clear to me or to many others here at Morris Champlin exactly how problematic homework could be for many of our students until Gregory forced us to look more closely at the overall situation. So while I cannot support any calls for a law restricting homework, I would definitely support our school forming a task force comprised of teachers, administrators, parents, and, yes, students to put their heads together and find solutions that work for all of us."

Later, Gregory realized that he heard Ana's "whoop" first, but at the time it seemed as though the entire student population in the auditorium cheered at once. Gregory was stunned, and photos Kay took at that moment showed eyes wider than they'd ever been.

"Gregory," Dr. Bankster continued, "I would like you to have the final words in this conversation this evening. I do not know if my suggestion is possible or if it achieves your goals, but since we are here only because of your passion and determination, I cede the floor to you."

Dr. Bankster left the podium to great applause. Or maybe, as Dr. Bankster said as they passed each other onstage, the applause was for Gregory coming to the podium. Either way, it took Gregory a few moments to regain his composure at the microphone. As he shifted from leg to leg and shook out his arms, he quickly ran through the options in his head. He was still on strike.

He didn't have to stop. But maybe Dr. Bankster was right? Or . . . ? He cleared his head and spoke from his heart.

"Thank you, Dr. Bankster. This whole strike has taught me a lot, including never to make assumptions about old city council meeting notes." Gregory took a deep breath. "A task force that includes students would be a great place to start, as long as we knew that the task force's recommendations would actually matter and not just be a way to make us disappear. In other words, it's good with me if it lets our voices be heard."

The rest of the gathering was a blur to Gregory. Principal Macallan agreed to form a committee and asked Dr. Bankster and Gregory to be the first two members. Crowds of kids swarmed him after the event, separating him from his parents and Kay. At one point, he was even hoisted onto the shoulders of the crowd like the winning quarterback after a big game.

Eventually, the crowd thinned out as people's attention turned back to the mundane aspects of life—getting home, meeting friends, and, of course, finishing homework.

Gregory worked his way from the far side of the auditorium back over to his family. His parents were deep in conversation, and as Gregory drew closer he realized they were talking with Kelly's mom. Just beside them, Alex, Ana, Benny, and Kelly were laughing and talking as if they'd known each other forever, even though Ana and Kelly had never met before.

It was Ana who saw Gregory first. "You did great!" She ran over and hugged her friend. "Is the strike over?"

"Yeah, I think it is," Gregory said. "Principal Macallan made it sound like the task force would happen soon. And, you know what? If it doesn't happen, we can always strike again."

Alex snapped a photo. "So, can I have exclusive interviews from the inside of the task force room?"

"If I speak, I promise it will be to you." Gregory and Alex exchanged high fives. Alex snapped a photo of their hands colliding.

"You're going to be exceedingly busy," Benny said. "I hope you can still do homework with us."

"You're back?" Gregory asked happily.

"Yes. I told my mother that I was going to join you. Period. My mother then decided you were not a bad influence. Just youthfully enthusiastic," Benny said. "I chose not to argue with her."

Finally, Gregory stood facing Kelly. The two hugged like the old friends they were. "Thanks for coming," Gregory whispered. Kelly kicked him in the calf.

"Did you think there was a chance I wouldn't, Gregory K.? And you were fantastic, by the way." Kelly held up a big brown paper bag. "I brought pies. So where do we go to get some milk in this town?"

Gregory's parents let everyone come over for a pie celebration. It was a festive group of friends, and O didn't try to steal anything from Gregory once, not even the world's greatest apple pie, freshly baked by Kelly's mom.

Despite having a long drive ahead of them, Kelly and her mother were the last to leave the Korenstein-Jaspertons' house.

"That was better than open mic night," Kelly said as they walked out toward the car.

"I think I still prefer poetry readings if you don't mind," Gregory said. "Like, a lot."

"So what's next, Gregory K.?" Kelly asked softly.

It only took a second for Gregory to respond. "Sleep. Weeks and weeks of sleep."

Hugs were exchanged all around, and smiles and laughs continued until Kelly and her mom drove away.

Gregory stayed outside after the rest of his family went in. The moonlight cast shadows through the trees, and he watched them move with the wind. He leaned against the wall on the porch, still unable to turn off his brain.

Was he right to end the strike? He'd never worked harder in his life on anything related to school, and the relief he felt about being done with the strike was genuine. At the same time, he'd never gotten more of his own work done during a school year . . . and his test scores were as good as they'd ever been. And the task force . . . well . . . it had potential. And it could matter. But it would be a lot of time spent and a lot of research to be done.

Gregory took a final look at sky and shadows, then headed inside to go to bed. There was too much to sort out, too many ands and buts. All he knew was that right now, he was exhausted, and tomorrow, he'd have homework.

All things considered, he was actually looking forward to it.

Author's Note

As Gregory K. discovered, the early 1900s were filled with homework battles across the United States. Many school districts limited or abolished homework, and in 1901 the California Civil Code was amended to include a prohibition of any "home study" by pupils under the age of fifteen anywhere in the state. The law was later repealed. Still, it is entirely possible that somewhere out there, there's a town or school district that never made their repeal official.

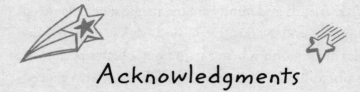

Acknowledgments

I was lucky enough to have many wonderful teachers, librarians and administrators during my years of school. Their kindness, knowledge, generosity (yes, Mr. Kurtz, Mr. Hamilton, and everyone at Lee—I'm definitely thinking of you), patience, and hard work helped give me the chance to find my voice. I am incredibly grateful to all of them and to all the teachers, administrators, and librarians working today and helping a new generation of students find their voices.

Once again, my appreciation goes to Arthur Levine for listening, pushing, prodding, reading, collaborating, and helping make this a better book and me a better writer. Thanks, too, to Weslie Turner for her feedback, ideas, and help in keeping me and *Strike* on track. And

I tip my hat to everyone at Arthur A. Levine Books and Scholastic for their fantastic work creating and supporting this book and *The 14 Fibs of Gregory K.* before it.

My friends and family are the magic sauce that keeps me going, and Nancy, Evan, and Myles, in particular, make me not only a better writer but a better person. It's not possible to thank them enough. I am also exceedingly grateful to Jon and Deborah for opening their house to me and letting me write, write, write. Huge thanks also go to Sara Wilson Etienne for the coffees, encouragement, and instant feedback at critical moments as this story took root . . . not to mention the years of friendship.

Finally, Mom and Dad—my first, longest-tenured, and most important teachers (and librarians and administrators, for that matter, and so much more)—thanks for . . . well . . . everything. And more specifically in terms of this book, thank you for always encouraging me and demonstrating to me the importance of finding my voice and letting it be heard. (Also, for the record, sometimes I actually didn't wash my hands when I said I did. I'm sorry. I don't do that anymore. Honest!)

Greg Pincus is a children's poet and novelist,
a screenwriter, and a social media strategist.
He is also an active member of the Society of
Children's Book Writers and Illustrators. He lives
in Los Angeles, California, and can be found online
at gregpincus.com and on Twitter as @GregPincus.

CAN'T GET ENOUGH GREGORY K?
Before The Homework Strike, there were...

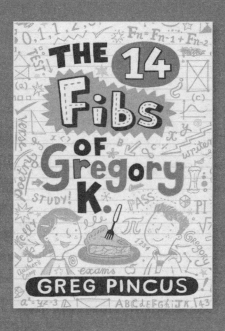

Gregory K. has been playing fast and loose with the truth: "I LOVE math" he tells his parents. "I've entered a citywide math contest!" he tells his teacher. "We're going to author camp!" he tells Kelly. And now, somehow, he's going to have to make good on all his promises.

"Exuberant and relatable, a winning equation."
—*Publishers Weekly*

ARTHUR A. LEVINE BOOKS
SCHOLASTIC

AALGREGK